ESCAPE

MARY
SANDERS
SMITH

MARICK
PRESS

Library of Congress Cataloguing in Publication Data

Mary Sanders Smith
Escape

ISBN 978-1-934851-11-1

Copyright © by Mary Sanders Smith, 2010
Design and typesetting by Sean Tai
Cover design by Sean Tai

Printed and bound in the United States

Marick Press
P.O. Box 36253
Grosse Pointe Farms
Michigan 48236
www.marickpress.com

Mariela Griffor, Publisher

Distributed by
Small Press Distribution
and
Wayne State University Press

Clawing up to the heights, headlong Pride
Crashes down the abyss—sheer doom!
No footing helps, all foothold lost and gone.

    – Sophocles: *Oedipus The King*

Nearly all men can stand adversity,
But to learn of a man's character,
Offer him power . . .

    – Attributed to Abraham Lincoln

GAVEL IN HAND, the court clerk pounds heavily on the table. "All rise."

The old courtroom groans as spectators shuffle to their feet. "The First District Court of Douglas County, Wisconsin, is now in session. Judge Peter Pearson presiding."

Get your stupid ass up, he tells himself. Or is it his lawyer speaking. Nothing matters anymore. Everything's locked in slow motion, sound, time. Carl Weston, Northwood State Prison Superintendent, is watching himself dissolve. He's had dreams like this where he's been unable to move, arms and legs heavy appendages, but he always woke up. Maybe he's going from one nightmare to the next.

All eyes focus on the judge as he lumbers into the courtroom. Floorboards complain beneath the weight of his blackrobed authority.

Judge Pearson speaks, a mouth forming silent words. The accused hears nothing until the gavel once again resounds throughout the courtroom. "Please be seated. Court is now in session."

Weston had not wanted a trial. "But what about justice?" his lawyer had argued. "Why do you insist on pleading guilty? I could help you. You have the right to be judged by your peers."

Peers? He has no peers.

Despondent, he lowers his head. Maybe his life had been headed in this direction all along, racing toward this very moment—to destroy him. The work that had given him so much pride was meaningless labor. He sees himself a dumb beast, nothing but flesh, a man with no purpose.

The courtroom fades and reappears in waves, drowning him. He struggles to regain a foothold as the river licks clean every rock within reach. All of his life Carl Weston had listened to the river, trusted its boundaries. It had betrayed him.

Gawkers fill the seats behind him. He thinks he saw some Indian relatives in the gallery. Supporters are transformed into enemies. Their leering pierces his back.

"Stand up straight," his lawyer hisses, "look the judge in the eye." He presses hard on each word. "It might lessen your sentence."

"Counsel," the judge asks, "has your client changed his mind?"

"No, your Honor, he insists on pleading guilty and is prepared for immediate sentencing."

The judge takes off his glasses, leans toward the defendant staring directly into his eyes. "Do you have anything to say at this time as to how the court should judge you?"

PRISON BREAK

THE ALARM BOOMERANGS through the prison hallways. Call the Superintendent! Inmates to their rooms! Call the Sheriff! Call in guards! Head count to see who's missing. Notify nearby homes to lock all doors. Report barking dogs.

"Hey, where's my watch?" "Go to your room." "I gotta' pee." "Go to your room." "My stuff's back there." "Go to your room."

Fake blanket roll under the covers. Fax inmate's base sheet—where from—fax escape to the county. Fax pictures to state and neighboring counties.

Jeffrey Brand would be long gone.

ONE

H E WISHED HE KNEW her full name. Who was this babe, anyway? Why was she doing this?

He memorized the note before burning it.

Still leery, Jeffrey Brand answered the girl's note. "I will do it," he wrote, not sure he actually meant it and placed it under the rock, prayed she would find it within the next two days. She must have, he thought, because she answered him that she'd be waiting for him. He had written her his final plan. The date was set.

Four days later, he woke long before the prison guards at Northwood State Minimum Security Prison forced the prisoners to get up. His heart pounded so hard he could see it. Over and over he rehearsed the escape. Just thinking the word made him shake.

By seven o'clock everyone was up. He stood in line with the other inmates for breakfast, as if he could swallow anything. No one talked to him since Dollar Bill had been sent back to maximum. As if it was his fault. Brand knew he'd been branded a snitch. He sat alone at the end of the table pushing eggs and grits in circles around his plate. Seconds dragged like hours. After chow, following his plan, he signed out for the Bull Gang and walked over to board the van. Just as they were about to pull out, he doubled over feigning pain.

"What's the matter?" the guard driving the van asked.

Brand gagged and doubled over in his seat.

"Better go to the infirmary," the guard said.

Brand walked toward the infirmary but stopped short of entering. Making sure the van had left, Brand went back to the annex to sign in at the library.

"Give up on the outdoors?" Jack asked as Brand entered the mobile unit.

"Got any jobs for me?"

"Sure, catalog these new books."

His plan was still on schedule. Brand settled in until Jack got busy with a couple of inmates on the computer. Keeping Jack in the corner of his eye, Brand studied the river map one last time. The whole picture looked even harder than he remembered. He stared at a jagged line that marked the river and the slashes that meant rapids. At least he understood where the Eau Claire River met up with the St. Croix. Several other streams entered the St. Croix downstream, but he wasn't sure how he'd recognize the Yellow River where he was to hole up for a couple of weeks. It looked to be a short way after a campground, but there were other campgrounds. Trouble was, it looked like a hell of a long ride. He'd absorbed about as much as he could and knew he had to get going.

Suddenly, Brand groaned and grabbed his gut. "I'd better go see the nurse," he told Jack.

He signed into the infirmary and waited in a chair.

"You look a little pale," the nurse said. "Better lie down on the cot."

Brand rushed for the toilet and faked vomiting, flushing repeatedly. A short time later, the nurse came to his cot and gave him some medicine.

"This should work for now," she said. "Come back if you feel worse."

He held the pill in the side of his mouth without swallowing, afraid it would put him to sleep.

"I think I'll go back to the annex now," he said. "Good thing I didn't go with the Bull Gang today."

"You'll be all right. Come back if it gets worse."

Brand spit out the pill. Everything was going smoothly until he rounded the corner and ran into the guard.

"Whoa!" Ryder said. "What are you doing here this time of day?"

Brand showed his release slips from the Bull Gang, the Annex and the infirmary. "I'm headed back to the annex," then grimaced and grabbed his gut.

Ryder checked out his paper work. " Maybe you should lie down for a while," Ryder said. "Hope you feel better."

Shit, Brand said to himself. This was not in the plan. He watched where Ryder headed so he could go in the opposite direction. Brand sauntered toward the front entrance, hoping no one in the office would see him. The secretary looked up and called to him.

"Where's your sign out?"

He tried to act calm. "I was sick and couldn't go on the Bull Gang—I tried to make it out in the annex. I went to the nurse, and now I'm going outside to get some air."

She looked at his papers, "Looks okay. Go ahead. Hope you feel better." He noticed she looked up at the clock and made a note.

She'd actually given him permission to go outside alone. He was so nervous that once outside, he threw up the little breakfast he'd eaten. He hoped she'd seen that through her office window.

Deciding it would be safer to exit out the back, he walked back through the building and made sure she watched him, waving as he passed the office door. Things were getting complicated. He headed toward the back exit that normally led to the annex.

Once outside, he scanned the grounds. No one was in sight. He walked as slowly as he could around the side of the building, trying not to look sneaky.

Wanting to run like hell, he moved in what seemed like slow motion, resisting the temptation to look behind. He had nothing but the clothes on his back. When he found the girl, everything would be waiting. She'd said so. He had to believe her. She'd said she loved him. Exhilaration raced through his arms. His legs tingled. Usually it took a couple of pops to feel this good.

Trying to walk not too far from the road but close enough to the tree line so he wouldn't be noticed, he reached the river and was more scared than when he'd been caught robbing the corner drug store.

The weather held nice and warm, trees all reds and yellows— as if he had any time to sit in the sun. He couldn't help feeling the color. He broke into a sweat. There was still time to turn around. Maybe the girl had devised some secret plot to catch him escaping, but the looming fourth conduct report kept him from turning back. The way he figured, he was doomed no matter what, get caught escaping or sent back to maximum if he stayed at prison. Didn't seem like much of a choice. Besides, a girl was out there waiting.

Leaving the prison camp boundaries, he followed her directions. Getting out of camp had been scarier than he'd imagined. There was no turning back. She'd written he'd have four hours before being missed if he followed her directions. Except for a few snags like running into Ryder, he'd done as she'd said.

He panted. His heart pounded relentlessly. He stopped to catch his breath just outside the prison camp grounds, hiding beneath alder shrubs. He shook so hard the leaves rattled. He'd never been this far from camp, out in the woods alone, except when he was on the Bull Gang, and even then he wasn't exactly alone. Trees and thick undergrowth were so rough that he couldn't see where he was headed. His mouth was pure cotton, and his knees felt like they belonged to some stranger. The river widened. Afraid he might be going in the wrong direction, he looked to follow the river, keep it to his left. He could barely see the water through the tangled forest. The shoreline was too wet to walk. Besides, he couldn't risk being seen from the road across the river. Anything could be hiding in here. He'd read that bears slept all day—he sure hoped so. He'd heard his share of bears growling at the garbage pit back of the prison in the middle of the night. Others claimed they'd seen them, but he'd never seen a bear there. He hoped he didn't wake one now.

The first time he heard fierce growls and snarls coming from the garbage pit, he imagined huge animals fighting each other. It reminded him of the human howls he'd heard at maximum. At least he wouldn't have to worry about bears once on the river.

He smiled to think he'd outsmarted Weston. Fuck the Superintendent. Weston hated him, that was for sure. But he couldn't figure why if Weston had hated him so much, he'd turned around and saved him from Dollar Bill. What the hell, he'd done it—he'd actually escaped. Well, almost. He wasn't quite on the river yet.

A rush like a first drag of grass propelled him. He hadn't bothered to stash any gear or weed, for that matter, in the woods. Just as well, nothing to weigh him down. Moving carefully, he stayed hidden, sneaking along like one of those creepy rats he'd watched along the Milwaukee River. He felt wild, just like a rat, answering to no one. Especially not to Weston.

The land was boggy underfoot. Exposed tree roots tripped him. He fell flat on his face. Stepping over and around brush and fallen logs was slow going, but now he needed to hurry. He prayed the girl was right about the four hours before he'd be missed. What if she wasn't there?

It took longer than he'd expected to reach the hydro dam, but once he saw it, he gained confidence. What the hell, he'd gotten this far. He tossed his head back and laughed at the sky. That shit Weston hadn't a clue.

Breathless from the steep incline, he reached the top of the stone embankment and slid down the left bank, just like she'd instructed, alongside where water cascaded from the dam into the narrow river. He swallowed hard at what faced him. Dumbfounded, he looked at the white water. Certain death. This had not been in the mix when he decided to escape. She hadn't told him the river was crazy all on its own, bouncing over and around boulders and fallen trees. He'd never get a canoe down this crap. He'd studied those slashes on the river map but had no idea that rapids would look this wild.

Beyond the dam, he walked the south bank like she'd directed. Thank God the river was getting deeper and wider. A rustle in the woods scared him. Sure it was a bear, he froze. Suddenly, a big buck, twice his size, jumped smack in front of him. The beast leapt across the river and instantly disappeared into the forest. His heart stopped. He'd never been so close to a wild animal, even when working the Bull Gang in the woods. It almost ran him down, for God's sake.

He still had a ways to go but sat down to catch his breath. He glanced around for more critters but couldn't keep his mind from racing back to the prison.

TWO

ON THE DAYS HE DIDN'T work the Bull Gang, he'd gone to the annex, returning again and again to the book on edible wild plants, reading up on how to survive if he could manage to escape. The more he learned, the more fascinated he became about living in the wild. He searched for these plants when he was out brushing on the Bull Gang. At first everything looked alike. One day he found some Queen Anne's Lace. The lacy blossom was easy to spot, and there was a ton of it. When the forest ranger came by to check their work, Brand asked him about it, and he was right. He had discovered Queen Ann's Lace. He'd read he could eat the roots so he grabbed a stem and easily pulled it from the sandy soil. The roots were small and rubbery. He couldn't bring himself to take a bite, but he sniffed it. Not too bad, earthy smelling.

"Hey, Curly, you don't gotta eat it, just kill it," Dollar Bill yelled.

"Get in the wind! I'd have to be really hungry to eat this crap," Brand yelled and tossed it on the ground.

"Just saving you, Curly, from death by poisoning."

Sundays were a big-time bore, but today turned out to be the perfect mid-summer's day to look for these so-called edible plants along the riverbank. At the prison, the Eau Claire River widened. Its water slowed and backed into eddies along the shore. It was more like a lake than a river. A couple of inmates were sitting in a rowboat, shirtless, floating in the middle of the river, fishing. On the opposite shore, Brand recognized cattails. Everywhere he went now, he searched for plants he'd seen in the book. Prisoners weren't allowed to cross beyond mid-point in the river even in a boat. He walked along the prison-side of the shore as far he as he was allowed and found a few more cattails. From what he'd read they were plentiful along streams. Until a few weeks ago, he didn't even know there was such a thing as a cattail. Now he knew it contained a bulb below water level that was edible and tasted like a cucumber.

He'd looked around for a safe spot to stash supplies he would need for an escape on the river, but the more he thought about it, the more discouraged he became. It was scary staring into this water so dark he couldn't see the bottom, probably over his head. He didn't know about water, let alone rivers. He'd never learned to swim.

One day he found some maps of the Eau Claire, St. Croix, and the Yellow Rivers in the library. It looked as though he could canoe down the Eau Claire, then down the St. Croix until he found where the Yellow joined, then paddle up the Yellow a bit and hide out in the woods for a couple of weeks eating wild plants until the authorities gave up on him. Sounded simple enough. He noticed an X mark on the flowage part of the St. Croix above the dam. In tiny print it said: *Ancient Indian Village*. Brand was intrigued. Maybe he could find it.

He'd memorized where the rivers joined, but once he put the map down, he couldn't keep it all straight in his mind. They looked just as foreign each time he went back to look. So what if he knew about certain wild plants to eat. Who was he kidding? He had no plan, no equipment, like a canoe for God's sake. Where would he find that? Steal one? He was losing resolve.

He was on his knees examining a plant he'd never seen before when one of the inmates fishing in the middle of the river gave a yell. He had a fish on his line and was screaming and laughing his head off. More than halfway across the river was off limits because a road ran along the river on the far side. Brand ran to the end of the dock to watch as the inmate's pole bent double. The action continued for twenty minutes or more before he finally brought the fish to the boat and his partner lifted it with the net. Brand was impressed.

Booker walked up as the whopper was hauled in the boat.

"Hey, let's go fishing," he said to Brand.

"I'm game, man."

They hurried back to the main building to sign out fishing rods and a boat. It was late in the afternoon, but Booker assured him that the fish bite better in the evening. They had a couple of hours before supper. Trouble was they had to dig their own worms.

"That won't take long," Booker said. "There's a spot out near the garbage pit where the guys dig them."

Finally they got their stuff in the boat, oars in the oarlocks, life jackets and all and rowed toward the exact spot where the men had caught the fish.

"Careful not to go past the middle," Booker warned Brand who manned the oars.

"Don't the hell I know that," Brand snapped as the boat shot this way and that.

"Let me row, Asshole," Booker said and shoved Brand aside.

Brand crawled to the front seat, hanging onto the sides of the boat, afraid they were about to tip over. Brand would never admit he couldn't swim, figured he'd grab a life jacket and hang onto the boat if they tipped over. The idea of escaping on the river was looking less appealing.

Booker handed Brand a pole. "You gotta bait your own hook."

"Huh?"

"Put your own worm on, stupid. You never gone fishin' before? Your folks never took you fishin'? Man, sometimes that was all we got to eat."

"Who hasn't gone fishing?"

"You Indian, ain't you?"

"Half, what's it to you?"

"Me, too, I'm half Indian, the other half is black. What's your other half?"

Brand shrugged. "You been in too long."

"Too long to suit me. I'm lookin' for a way to cut."

Brand ignored him, smart talk just like the rest of them waiting to hit the bricks. He jiggled his bait and scanned the shoreline for edible plants, but he was too far from the shore to see anything specific. Something grabbed his line and took off. Brand reeled as the fish jumped in the air. "Whoa," he yelled. "Look at that beauty!" He didn't know one fish from another and reeled in harder. Suddenly the line went limp.

"You lost it, you asshole. You don't even know how to catch a fish."

"Shut up. It wasn't my fault."

They waited a while longer without any action. The sun hung above the pines on the west shoreline.

Booker seemed nervous. "We better go chow down."

After eating Brand went to watch TV, but nothing good was on, and the rest were snow stations. He decided to go look for Dollar Bill to play catch. He caught up with him back at the room. They were on their way out to the ball field when the escape alarm went off.

Weston's voice boomed over the intercom. "All inmates go directly to your rooms. Stop all activity. Proceed directly to your rooms. This is a lock down."

"Must be a false alarm," Dollar Bill said walking as slowly as he could down the hall.

"Step it up," Ryder warned.

All the exterior doors automatically locked. Dollar Bill and Brand slumped onto their cots. "Wonder how long this will last," Brand grumbled.

Ryder stuck his head in the door. "Brand, you're wanted in Superintendent Weston's office immediately."

"Me? What did I do?"

Brand sauntered into Weston's office.

"Sit down, Brand. I want to talk to you."

"What did I do?"

"I'm going to find out. Booker has left the grounds, escaped. You were last seen with him."

"I don't know nothing. We were just fishing, that's all. I came in to mess hall. I never saw him after we put the boat away."

"Did he say anything to you? Ask you to help him?"

"No, Mr. Weston, I swear, I don't know nothin.'"

"That's all, Brand. Stay in your room until we announce all's clear."

There was nothing to do but go to bed. Dollar Bill was playing solitaire. Brand lay on his cot hating Booker for hooking him into this. He had enough problems of his own. Around midnight the all-clear alarm sounded.

At breakfast he heard that Booker had been caught. No one would sit by Brand at mess, not even Dollar Bill.

Lucky passed him and hissed, "Snitch!" in his ear.

Brand got up and went over to where Lucky sat. "What's that all about?"

"As if you didn't know. They caught Booker after you spilled to Weston where he went. We know you was fishin' with him."

"Yeah, so what? Where'd they get him?"

"Walking down the railroad tracks."

"Dumb shit. I never said nothing to Weston. Booker deserved to be caught if he was stupid enough to escape that way." But he knew they didn't believe him and wanted someone to blame.

THREE

THEY HAD CAUGHT BOOKER, but they wouldn't catch him. At last Brand spotted the yellow ribbon on a tree as the girl had promised in her note. It marked her cabin along the river bank. Set well back in a grove of tall trees, the cabin was surrounded by a thick cover of pine needles that blanketed the ground giving rise to a sweet pungent smell swirled about by a warm breeze. He'd never thought much about perfect days, but this held rank. Tapping on the back door, he was afraid she wouldn't answer. Suddenly, there she was, long black hair and all.

It had been forever since he'd been so close to a girl.

"Quickly," she said. "There's a canoe, your gear, food, everything's in the canoe. You must hurry. There's not much time before they will sound the prison alarm."

This was the first time he'd heard her speak.

"Hey, come here," he smiled and reached for her hand and drew her to him. "How do you know all this—how to escape and all? Why are you doing this?"

"Never mind." She took his face in her hands and kissed him. "You taste good."

She urged him toward the river, pulling him along by the hand.

"Not so fast, I need another kiss."

"Have you forgotten?" she giggled. "You're escaping from prison."

He spotted the canoe pulled on shore all ready to go.

"Where did you get all this stuff?"

"Never mind."

Her kiss was as soft as her voice, and he wanted more, but suddenly he was afraid to touch her.

"Your eyes—my eyes. I love you, Matt."

"What? What's this Matt shit?"

"Never mind. What's your name? "

Brand grinned. "Jeff."

"Jeff, Jeff," she repeated. "You must hurry."

'No way," and he pulled her against his chest. He kissed her hard, pressing against her body.

"Oh, yes," Brand grunted as he rubbed his groin against her.

She squirmed from his grasp.

"You must go. You don't have much time."

Brand grabbed her once again.

"I put some money in the pack. Promise you'll return someday? I live on road G out of Northwood, same as the prison, right next to the river."

"Whatever you say," he said kissing her and then forced her back toward the cabin.

"What are you doing? Are you crazy? You have to get out of here."

"First things first," he said as he pulled her against him and began kissing her from the neck down.

She pushed him away.

"You said you loved me," he said. "Prove it."

"No, no, you have to go—right now!"

He managed to get her back to the cabin, opened the screen door and pulled her into the kitchen.

"You're crazy!" she laughed.

"For you," he moaned.

"What if my father comes home?" She pulled away from him and ran behind the kitchen table.

"Father?" he yelled. "You never said you had a father!"

"Everyone has a father."

"Not me!"

"You better get out of here fast," she screamed. "Don't you understand?"

He lurched across the table at her.

Her hand crashed into the side of his face.

"What the fuck!" he grabbed his head. "You some kind of karate wrestler?"

She pointed to the clock on the wall. "Look—now you only have a few hours to get down the river where you'll be safe."

"Where's that?" he asked.

"I told you. When you reach the mouth of the Yellow River, it will be tomorrow, maybe the next night. You'll recognize it. It looks yellow and is large where it enters the St. Croix water. Paddle up a way and disappear with the canoe into the woods for a couple of weeks. You'll be safe there." She paused and stared into his black eyes.

He walked around the table locked in her gaze. "Don't be frightened." He enveloped her with his body. "You want to?"

She didn't answer him with words, but he thought her eyes said yes.

She took his hand and led him back to the river. He followed her like a tamed sheep.

She leaned forward to kiss him good-bye, but he turned away.

"Damn you," he said as he stepped into the canoe and almost tipped over.

"Hey, dummy, never stand up in a canoe. Put a hand on each side when you crawl to the bow or stern." She pushed him into the stream, bow first. "Got it?"

He tried to smile but was too scared.

"Go fast," she called as he grappled with a canoe paddle for the first time in his life. "I forgot," she yelled after him. "If you tip over, hang onto the canoe—never let go of the canoe."

He nodded with his back to her, and when he looked around to find her again, he'd already swept around a bend. She was out of sight.

Brand could not believe this was happening—the Dollar Bill shit—Booker's escape—the girl, and now—his escape. He was so fucking lucky.

At first, he fought the water as the canoe careened from one side of the stream to the other, jamming into one overhanging bush after another. He imagined her watching and laughing at him. This Matt thing raced in and then right out of his mind. As the water slowed, he turned the paddle ever so slightly, and discovered the canoe yielded to his touch, first to the right, then left. Less was best. He stroked the velvety smooth water that reminded him of the shiny new paint job on the hood of his uncle's stolen car. This was cool, even cooler than riding in the van with the windows open or hitting a home run. He forgot about the girl.

Just to think of escaping had been impossible, and yet here he was. He'd never had a high like this in his life. A wild ride. He didn't care if he lived beyond this moment. Best of all he'd outsmarted Weston.

This was the best moment he'd ever known, and if he played it right, it would never end. He would ride this current the rest of his fucking life, like a feather cresting the wind. Who cared what was around the next bend. He was free.

Freedom, Brand repeated to himself. Out here where nobody expects anything of him—where there's nothing they can take from him. Now that's freedom, he thought.

FOUR

BEFORE HE KNEW IT, he'd zipped right on through Northwood, under the County Road Bridge, floated past the cemetery and almost forgot he'd ever been a prisoner or a fish getting his stripe. He scanned the water's edge, the trees, the brush, searching for edible plants, disappointed he couldn't recognize any of the plants he'd read about. At least he wasn't worried about bears here in the middle of the river.

A whoosh swooped from a tree. He ducked, almost falling out of the canoe. He'd never seen a bird that big. Must be an eagle. He'd read about them and seen pictures in the nature books in the library. Warning cries carried aloft. It screeched with a shrill a much smaller bird might make and flew on ahead, carefully blocking a clear view of itself behind several pines before landing atop a tall tree. He thought a bird that big would make a louder squawk.

He wished he had wings. It would make it easier. He'd never felt free before, and it was so good—sooo fucking good—it hurt. As long as he could remember, he'd been running, but this was different. Even if he got caught, they'd never dare punish him after what Dollar Bill did to him. He'd sue for his rights. But he wasn't going to get caught.

Good thing he'd found those river maps in the prison library and had memorized the layout. Now he knew what he had to do. He would cruise down the St. Croix to the Yellow River, paddle up a way and hide in the woods for a couple of weeks until they called off the hunt. Now that he understood the slashes on the map stood for rapid water, it should be exciting. Besides he hadn't seen too many on the map.

He'd heard it said the prison guards only searched hard the first twenty-four hours, then left it up to the state police. The state police didn't search the immediate area. No one would think to look for him in the woods or along the river since most escapees took to the roads to catch a ride or steal a car. Or they'd walk the railroad like that asshole Booker when he tried to escape.

He noticed small houses spotted along the river, but no one was around. Some looked empty, maybe the time of year. Ahead was a fork in the river. It scared him to think he might make the wrong turn, but once he moved closer he saw he was joining another river. Must be the St. Croix, he thought, recalling the map, and he paddled around the curve following the current that led under the railroad bridge. The next bridge was clearly a highway with plenty of traffic, mostly speeding trucks. There was no headroom, and he was zipping right toward it. At the last minute, he flattened himself in the canoe as the bottom of the bridge almost brushed his nose. He looked back at what he'd floated under and couldn't believe he'd made it. This was a cinch.

And Ryder had said he couldn't think beyond his nose. Here he'd just pulled off the best escape in the last century. Weston would be sweating it out big time. Served him right, calling him in to his office, making him out to be a snitch.

Next came the swampy part the girl had mentioned. He wished he knew her name. He'd forgotten to ask. She always signed her name "E." He was sorry he swore at her, but she'd gotten him all excited and then wouldn't do it.

Tall reeds covered most of the expanse, but the river's path was obvious, and he paddled hard, feeling totally exposed in this open area where anyone driving by on the highway could spot him. He headed toward the bank covered by trees with white bark, blanketed by shimmering yellow leaves. The river must turn west here, judging from the sun. It was pretty, he had to admit. This must be what a vacation is like. He'd never been on a vacation, not a real one that was planned where you went somewhere fun. The only vacation he remembered was when he was little, and that was summer vacation from school. It was horrible because he was all alone in one room with his mom gone all day who the hell knew where. When he braved it outside, he had to run like crazy to steal food or escape from the big boys.

Brand reared back and laughed out loud. This had to be what heaven was like. Tall reeds that rolled in the breeze looked like the wild rice he'd seen in the plant book in the library. But he couldn't waste time gathering wild rice. The girl had told him to stick to the river shore once he headed west.

This was cool, he thought. He sensed he'd been here before, maybe the memory had disappeared at some point in his past and was back for a visit. It felt weird as though he belonged here.

Once he rounded the next bend, the river was easy going with gently flowing water. Its varnished surface belied a steady current below as Brand watched bottom grasses swinging and swaying in a gentle rhythm. His arms were tired, but he dared not let up. He counted on baseball practice and clearing all that brush to get him in shape.

A bird planed in a lazy circle high above him. Must be the same eagle that spooked him. Maybe it was following him.

He couldn't stop looking at the yellow trees with the white trunks. They were endless along with so many plants on the riverbank. He wanted to stop and examine them, desperately wanted to know their names. Nobody in his world had real names, just pick up stuff. He didn't even know the girl's name. It was her fault—she should have told him. He wished he'd studied that wild plant book more, memorized names of poisonous as well as edible ones. But then he figured before no one was here, these plants had no names either. So why should he give a shit. The river widened into a shallow lake, and he stuck to the shoreline like she'd told him.

Maybe this was where the ancient Indian village had been. From what he could tell that he'd seen on the map, it had to be somewhere along here. He tried to imagine what it would be like to be an Indian in the wilderness. Must have been tough. They must have lived like animals out here.

The sky was clouding up. He was glad he no longer needed the sun for direction. Now he could just follow the river. He looked at his watch. Pretty soon they'd find he was missing, maybe not quite yet. It would be one hell of a loud sound. It excited him to think of it, and he paddled harder.

He spotted the CCC dam ahead that the girl had described. He'd seen it on the map, too. He'd have to pull the canoe out here and put in on the downriver side. No problem. He was getting expert at this river stuff. As he approached the dam, the wind picked up from the west. He was glad he was through the lake part and didn't have to paddle into all that wind. A sign said the dam was built in 1936. That was before his mom was even born, as if she gave a shit about him. He hadn't heard a word from her in years. On one side there was a camp site. He would have to pull his canoe past it. Luckily, it was deserted. He had an urge to walk across the dam to the other side of the river, but didn't dare take the time. Some day he'd come back and camp here with his girl.

The prison would look for him here for sure if they figured out he was on the river. The wind was whipping around now, but he wasn't worried. He could handle it. The river was shallow and moving right along downstream below the dam. Wind shouldn't be a problem.

A couple of times the canoe got hung up on flat rocks where it was shallow, but he was able to push off. All of sudden, he felt cold blasts even though he was paddling hard. The sky was loaded like a white sponge as clouds rolled in on themselves. He reached in the plastic bag to find something warmer, grabbed a rain slicker and thought any other time he would never let himself be seen in this. Who the hell would see him out here?

He paddled right along. A big fish jumped in front of the canoe. It must have been trapped against a rock as he floated up on it. He'd never seen a fish jump like that, maybe two feet in the air. Too bad he didn't have a fishing rod. Some guys spent hours out in the row boat fishing, but he never saw anyone catch a fish that big. It was even bigger than the one he lost when he went fishing with Booker before Booker's big escape. Brand laughed. Some escape. Booker should see him now. It took some brains to pull this off.

The scenery was getting better and better, but the wind was blowing harder now, and the sky to the west didn't look so good either, dark and threatening, as though night was marching upon him before its time. No sign of the bird. As though from nowhere, suddenly came snow—and with a fury, not just one flake at a time. What a crazy country, hot one minute, snow the next. Back in Milwaukee they were lucky to have snow by Christmas. Just last weekend he'd been sweating in a tee shirt.

Trees bent double under the sudden onslaught. The ones with white bark grazed the ground, whipping back and forth like crazy in total obedience to the fickle wind. Blinded by the snow, he knew he had to keep going. How could everything change so drastically from summer to winter? He'd never known anything like this. He'd gone from shirt sleeves to a rain suit in a matter of minutes and wondered how long this storm would last. He studied the sky. It looked serious, and it worried him.

Suddenly, a roar surfaced above the storm. White water frothed in front of the canoe. Good thing he had the rain suit on. He struggled to paddle and steer at the same time. The water wound like a rope waiting to be cinched. First, the canoe hit a rock on one side, glanced sideways, then backward, hit a rock on the other side and lunged forward. He heard a crack as a log fell smack in front of the canoe. Instantly, he was thrown into the surging water as the canoe hit the log. He struggled to get his footing in waist deep water. Luckily it wasn't over his head, and the canoe hadn't tipped over. His gear was still with him. He clung to the canoe, got his balance and maneuvered toward shore. It was deeper there, but he managed to grab a bush and pulled himself partway out of the water without losing his grip on the canoe. He edged himself over to the boggy bank and stared at the river. At least he hadn't lost the garbage bag with his belongings, or the paddle, or gotten wet above the armpits. There had been no time to be scared, but now he was afraid. That log hadn't hit him, but he had been thrown into the water. What if he'd lost the canoe?

He looked around him and saw he was sitting on an island dominated by tall pines. One big one had fallen next to a crude fire pit, and he pictured people picnicking. He would love a fire right now but hadn't the time. He hoped the girl had put matches in his garbage bag. The longer he stayed, the less he wanted to get back on the river. Getting back in the canoe with all this water whizzing past him would be a challenge.

Snow swirled and whipped its way upstream, momentarily caught in foam that spit forth from a skittering spray and circled boulders like animals closing in on their prey. Time had stopped within these arcs racing round and round. Where had it come from, this iron roar of swiftness that had dumped him in its midst?

He managed to dump water from the canoe and quickly hop in. Once back in the canoe, steering this way and that, he worked his way around each rock that confronted him, as he plummeted down the rapid water. At the bottom of the rapids, he sat for a minute in the calmer water and looked back at the clutter of rocks blocking the passage. He'd come upon the island so fast and could have gone to the right or left. He must have taken the wrong way. White water coiled about each rock, spraying foam every which way. He couldn't believe he'd survived with everything intact. On a hot summer day this might be fun, but he hoped he'd seen the worst. Nothing could stop him now.

There was no time to waste. The storm was worsening, and it was getting darker. They must be after him by now. At least he didn't have to worry about bears. Nothing would be out in this crappy weather.

God, how he envied this river. It had been here forever— what power—harnessed and directed by its banks. So that's what power was all about—control. Spread out, it would fizzle.

FIVE

EVIE HAD WATCHED JEFF struggle with the canoe to round the bend. She gave him a thumbs up but knew he hadn't seen her. She had no idea if she would ever see him again. But if he did have her brother Matt's spirit within him, he would return to her. He'd asked her why she was doing this for him? She just knew she had to, that's all. Part of it was about freeing Matt's spirit. Her dad would call her crazy. She may be trapped here in her dad's world, but at least she'd done her part to free Jeff.

She'd skipped school to help him escape and now didn't know what to do with the time on her hands. At noon she decided to go back for afternoon classes.

"So where have you been?" Ann Marie said as Evie walked into the cafeteria.

"Visiting my ancestors," Evie said.

"Oh, I get it—no questions allowed, right?"

Evie feigned innocence.

All afternoon Evie imagined what Jeff was going through. She knew the river well enough to picture him fighting his way through each rapid. Thank goodness it was a beautiful day. When she walked to the parking lot after her last class, Evie checked out the sky and saw dark clouds building to the west. By the time she arrived home, the sky to the west was looking ominous. Once in the house, she wished she had her spirit friend, Ann Marie's, rabbit blanket to kneel on and pray for Jeff's safety. Instead, she went down to the river but couldn't stand to imagine his tipping over and emerging from cold water to an even colder temperature. She was getting too cold to stay here any longer as the wind picked up. She imagined him freezing to death this very night, and it would be all her fault.

She thought she heard the prison alarm but knew it was just nerves because she couldn't hear that far away, especially with the wind picking up from the west. She went up to her room and crawled into her bed convincing herself she had done the right thing. She imagined when he would return to her. They would marry and finish school. They would make contact with her Indian relatives on the reservation in Hayward, perhaps live with them and recreate their Indian heritage. Their children would be more Indian than either of them. They would go ricing in the fall and make maple sugar and syrup. They would spear fish in the spring, grow their food in the summer and live off the land. They would belong to each other and their native American roots. It made perfect sense.

Her friend, Ann Marie, had acted like Evie was committing a crime when she'd told her about helping the prisoner. The crime, Evie thought, would be not to help him. She was freeing his spirit.

Evie still had some relatives living on the Court Oreilles reservation. She'd neglected those families since her mother died but remembered her mother taking her and Matt to various events on the reservation. She'd always loved going there and felt guilty thinking she'd abandoned them. It angered her to think her father hadn't made sure they stayed in contact. Now that she thought about it, he'd made a conscious effort to keep her from her Indian relatives.

One summer her mother had taken her to a ceremonial dance following the fall harvests of rice and maple sugar.

Wearing their best beaded clothing the Indians reenacted the harvesting rituals through dancing and drum beating. Evie thought it looked like fun, but she was little then and didn't understand what it all meant.

Since then her Spirit Club had read about various ceremonial dances, and she decided to find out when she could go watch one at the reservation. Dances were held for almost any occasion, harvesting, births, deaths, war parties and victories. Then there were the scalping dances, but surely that wasn't done anymore. The woman's dance interested her. It must have been the dance she saw with her mother because she remembered only women dancing. At first she'd been scared because they jumped from side to side in groups and leapt toward her. That's the one she wanted to see again.

Her wild thoughts kept her from falling asleep, so she got up and went downstairs to start supper. She didn't know if her dad would come home once the escape alarm sounded but knew he'd have a fit if she didn't have dinner ready.

SIX

IT COULDN'T HAVE COME at a worse time. Maybe it was the
lunch, maybe the constant fights with his daughter Evie. Bent
over double, Superintendent Weston downed some medicine,
shook off his dizziness, then stood and pulled up his pants.

His pager sounded. Code five, code five repeated over the
intercom. There hadn't been a successful escape in twenty years,
and now here were two attempts in one summer. He ran back
to his office. Who could it be, he wondered, thumbing through
the list of prisoners.

The alarm blasted. "Damn," he said and pounded his desk.
He'd counted on making it through to retirement without this.
The alarm pulsed through his brain. This was major.

When he heard it was Brand, he freaked out. "Goddamn
stupid kid! Might have known!" There went his career record of
zero escapes.

He proceeded according to the rules. Don't outsmart yourself, he thought. The search would spread out on the roads, the
railroad tracks, the small roads leading to cabins in the area.

Gather the inmates, search the escapee's room, inform local
police, inform state police.

"Where did you last see him?" Weston pressed the inmate in
the room next to Brand.

"Breakfast."

"What did he say?"

"Nothin.'"

Weston had had serious reservations about Brand from the start, the arrogance, the insolance. Those deep brown eyes knew another world. The more he thought about him, the more it angered him. Brand's roommate, Dollar Bill, was back at the wall, and no one else knew Brand except Jack.

"He was quiet and polite at the annex," Jack said. "But beneath it all I suspected anger."

"What did he do here?"

"I think he was always figuring out how to escape. He never settled in although he did his school work. He read nature books. I already told you that."

"So?—think!"

"Oh, yeah, he studied maps—river maps. I didn't even know we had them, but somehow he found them in books."

It had been a long time since anyone had tried to escape on the river system. None had made it. They usually took to the road. He tried to remember if Brand had used the boats here at camp. He checked the boat sign up forms and found Brand's name signed up with Booker just before Booker had tried to escape.

He rifled through Brand's belongings. Nothing unusual in his trunk, a few clothes, some hard candy, his baseball mitt, no notes or maps. The only clue he had about Brand was his unusual interest in wild plants. On one of Brand's visits on demand to Weston's office, he'd told Weston his cousin had a company dealing in environmentally safe foods and wanted to hire him. Weston never bought into it, and there was no evidence of that in his foot locker. Maybe Brand had escape in mind all along, and Dollar Bill had tipped the scales. But what was with the wild plants? Survival perhaps.

Local authorities had all the information now, but nothing

surfaced. The sheriff's police would scour the immediate roads and houses for the next twenty-four hours.

"What's going on, Ryder? Any news?"

"Everyone in the state system has been alerted. No word yet. The weather doesn't look too good. They're predicting an Alberta Clipper."

"I never listen to weather reports—ten miles north, a mile south, never on target."

"If we go after him on the river, no one can do that alone. I'll call in Peterson. He's retired, but he'll help out."

"I'll need all the help I can get if I go on the river." Weston knew he wasn't coming clean with Ryder. He didn't mention how Brand reminded him of his son, Matt, and how that made him mad as hell. The resemblance was uncanny. Brand had already ruined Weston's no-escapes career record. But duty came first. "I know this kid. I'll catch him," Weston said. "I'll call you when I get him."

You bet he would get him. He would never forget that Brand, a loser, was alive and Matt was dead.

Weston jumped in his truck and headed along the river for his place. Evie was home getting supper.

"I won't have time to eat—business to attend to," Weston said. He collected his foul weather gear and grabbed his pistol. "Any one strange been around?"

"Why?"

"Prison escape, half-Indian named Brand."

"You should eat before you leave."

Weston checked his watch and dropped his gear to the floor. "Good idea, besides I'd better wait for another state police report. Maybe they found him on the road. Sure hope so." He left the kitchen to down some medicine to calm his riling gut.

"Where are you going to search?" Evie asked as she scooped spaghetti onto a plate.

The spaghetti didn't look too appetizing, but he knew he had to eat something. "I'll start with houses along the river. State police cover the highways."

"Should I be scared?"

"Damn right. Lock the doors and don't answer the door for anyone even if you think you know them." He pushed his plate of spaghetti aside, leaving half. "Good spaghetti, Evie."

"So I see," she snapped.

The phone rang, and Evie jumped to answer it.

"I don't want you going anywhere tonight," Weston called to her.

"I'll call you back," Evie said to the caller.

"Who was that?"

"Ann Marie—math homework."

"Call her back, but don't go out of house, and don't answer the phone anymore after I leave, okay?"

"I guess," Evie snapped. "I hate your job!"

"It feeds us—anyway, I'm about to retire."

"Thank God."

"I'll feed Precious when I get back. Don't you go outside. Hear me?"

"How could I not hear you. You're shouting."

"I'm sorry, Evie," and he gave her a kiss before she could turn away.

Weston made a quick call to Ryder on his cell phone. Officer Peterson was home sick. There was no news of a capture or sightings, so he grabbed his gun and gear before heading out to his pickup. It would be dark in a few minutes. This was the last thing he wanted to do, chase a no-good loser in a storm. A cold wind freshened and whipped the trees. Something stopped him from starting the engine. He walked to the river and then over to Clarence's place next door. Everything looked normal, but his gut told him to check their communal canoe rack. He saw only three canoes. One was missing.

"That you, Carl?" Clarence peered out his back door. "Wondered who was out there."

"It's okay, Clarence, notice any stranger around this afternoon?"

"We weren't home, up at the doctor's in Superior. What's up?

"Canoe's missing from the rack."

Clarence hobbled out to look. "Sure 'nough."

"There's been a prison escape. Keep your doors locked."

"Will do. Thanks, Carl. Hope you catch him."

Weston hurried back to his truck to call Ryder. "Any news?"

"Nothing."

"Canoe's missing here. Paddle, too. I'll check some more places on the river, and if nothing turns up, I'm heading down the river."

"Storm's headed this way, might be an Alberta Clipper," Ryder warned. "You can't go alone. I will find someone else to go with you."

"Suits me, but I don't have much time to waste."

"I'll try to get a hold of Nick Bremmer. He's a forest ranger and in good shape."

"Yeah, I remember him. Call me right back."

Weston missed his fishing pal, Ole. He would have gone with him, storm or no storm.

Weston knew if Brand had escaped on the river in this storm, especially if it did turn out to be an Alberta Clipper, it could drop five, seven feet of snow, even more within twenty-four hours. Storms like this kill people. All the same, much as he hated Brand, he would go after him even if it meant going alone. No one could ever accuse him of not doing his job. Besides, Brand was inexperienced and should be easy to find.

A search of the houses between his place and Northwood produced nothing. No one had seen or heard a thing, and he traced his way back to his place. Joe Krug stood at the door shaking his head. "Weston, you're a crazy fool! Out in this weather."

Weston grabbed his cell phone. "That you Ryder? What did you find out?"

"Found Nick Bremmer. Says he'll be waiting for you at the Northwood Bridge. He can help you check cabins for a break-in."

"Sounds good. Tell him I'm shoving off right now."

There was no urgency now except for the storm. If Brand were on the river, he wouldn't get far. Even without a major storm, the odds were against him. Maybe a couple had made it before Weston's time, now that he thought about it, but none in a storm.

Convinced now that Brand had escaped on the river, Weston pulled his canoe from the rack, angrily snapped in the center seat, tossed his gear in front of the gunnel, secured it and shoved off. Snow began to fall as the canoe glided into the current. Thank God his stomach had calmed down.

Paddle in hand, Weston relaxed as the canoe responded to his command. He was back home. Many a black night in spring, summer or fall he'd cruised the Eau Claire and St. Croix rivers, fly rod in hand, knowing every curve and rock like a friend. He might not control the weather, but he had a handle on the river.

The spring-fed Eau Claire sported trout, but by the time it blended into the warmer St. Croix, fed by tributary streams—no longer underground springs, the fishing changed to black bass with an occasional walleye or northern pike. A fly rod was still the order of the day, but the bait changed from a small hand-tied fly to a hair frog. He laughed remembering Ole's story. Poor Ole, experienced as he was, something was always happening to him.

He wondered how in hell Brand would ever maneuver these waters with no experience. If he *was* on the St. Croix, and Weston's gut feeling convinced him he was, Brand had better get lucky. Odds were he'd flip like Ole in the first rapids at Elizabeth Island. He'd know soon enough.

Memories of Elizabeth Island distracted him, and he thought about one mid-July hot, hot day when he and Matt had waded back into the boggy ponds a few hundred yards from the river and caught their limit of bass. The ponds had a boggy bottom. Casts had to be controlled because of overhanging underbrush. Matt knew how to cast a fly. Weston had made sure of that, but somehow that day, maybe it was the heat, maybe the mood, they both kept getting snagged on their back casts. After a while it was funny, and it became a game for the worst cast. Weston remembered purposely hanging up in an alder bush just for a laugh. Despite all that, they'd caught a ton of bass, tossing most back. Afterward, they'd trudged back to the island, hot to the bone, stripped and laid flat in the rapids hanging on to rocks for dear life. Suddenly a bear sow and her cub had appeared on the opposite shore. She didn't see them and started across the river just a few yards downstream. Normally the wind was out of the west which would put them downwind from the bear, but the wind was calm. He was worried, but she didn't pick up their scent. Knowing bears see well, they'd clung to the rocks holding their breath, and, sure enough, she trudged right through the rapids to the other bank, ignoring them, and stopped with her cub to eat blueberries.

Weston pulled in under the Northwood bridge and clung to a willow tree bent double to the stream, bobbing up and down as though dying of thirst. Bremmer should be here by now.

The wind picked up and snow stung his face, definitely from the west tonight, but then most storms came from the west or northwest. Funny how he remembered that hot day with his son Matt when it was getting so damned cold out here.

Weston would give Bremmer another few minutes. Finally, he called Ryder one last time.

"Bremmer's not here. It's been thirty minutes. No time to waste. I've made it through a lot of storms. I'll call when I find Brand, and you pick us up at one of the bridges on the St. Croix.

I'll let you know."

"Okay," Ryder said. "I'll tell Bremmer to meet you at the . . ." Ryder's phone broke up, and Weston couldn't hear where he said Bremmer would wait for him. Maybe he meant the Northwood Dam.

There were a few cabins after the bridge. Weston pulled into shore and crawled onto land to check the cabins. All three were dark and locked up tight.

It took another hour or more to get to the dam and portage around it. Bremmer was nowhere in sight. Weston decided to go it alone.

He had no trouble negotiating the Elizabeth Island rapids, shipping a little water over the bow as he bounced through waves created by the rocks and the drop. He knew to stay left of the island. Brand wouldn't know that. The right side looked tamer, but there was no channel and no possible entry back to the main channel. As the storm worsened, Weston back-paddled to drift as slowly as possible through the rapid water, shining his flashlight along each shore. The river slowed and widened after the rapids. He scanned the shorelines, but it was hard to see through the blinding snow and hard to judge how much had fallen. Brand might have decided to stop and rest, especially if he'd tipped over. Except for some fallen trees, logs and brush, nothing resembled a person.

He thought he might find Brand hung up on the shore below the next treacherous spot, Scott's rapids. Listed a number-three difficulty on the river map, Scott's rapids demanded canoeing skills far beyond a beginner. In comparison, Elizabeth Island rapids was a number-two. Not only were there huge rocks at Scott's rapids, but Weston knew it took a canoeist with ability far beyond Brand's to maneuver through and around the exposed and hidden boulders, all the while trying to hug the right shore, worming the canoe down the rapids between the boulders, before dropping into a pool of water fifteen-feet deep.

At the foot of Scott's rapids was a campsite where Weston and Matt had camped many times. Their main entertainment had been watching the few canoes that had made it this far tip over.

As he zipped through Scott's rapids, froth blew from the water's surface in the face of the storm. Weston managed to scan the edges of the river. The shoreline revealed nothing.

Weston pulled up to the campsite below Scott's Rapids to catch his breath and look around for Brand. He felt for his gun to make sure he still had it just in case Brand had somehow stolen a gun. If Brand had tipped over in Scott's rapids, he might have made it to this campsite. The DNR had a posted camping sign, providing Brand could see it through the snow. Weston rubbed a crick in his back. Thank God his stomach was still calm.

He remembered another stomach episode that was pretty funny one morning when he and Matt had camped here. Weston had disappeared into the woods in a hurry to use the open air toilet the DNR had recently installed. He'd found the lid open, but when he sat down, there were fresh bear feces at his feet. Pretty funny imagining a bear trying to use an open air port-a-potty. Back at their tent, he'd noticed their cooler had been dumped during the night by a bear searching for food.

Scanning the area, Weston found no sign that anyone had landed here tonight, but the snow was falling so fast any footprints would soon be covered. Obviously Brand wasn't here, and Weston needed to move on, but he hated to leave. It was as though the earth had folded over to start anew, formed a fresh crust to test a new pioneer. An owl screeched nearby, reminding him to get back on the river.

He decided to call Ryder once more to see what was happening and tell him where he was. "Find Brand?" The reception was bad.

"No word," Ryder faded in and out. "Careful—hell—of storm."

"I know, you don't have to keep reminding me—I'm in it—for Chrissake. Never found Bremmer." Weston hung up, not sure Ryder had heard him and pushed off into the stream.

Copper Mine Dam was the next real danger. Unless Brand knew the way through that seven-foot immediate drop, he would have to portage around the sluice dam left over from when the land was logged one hundred years ago. Not only was there the one big drop, but logs and spikes planted long ago made it too dangerous unless the water was extremely high. At best this passage was iffy. If Brand made it past Copper Mine Dam, it didn't get much easier from there on either because large boulders lay hidden beneath the water's surface. Weston had learned them the hard way. Once a canoe mounted one of those beauties, it was doomed.

Weston paused to zip his foul-weather suit up to his chin. From here, it was a two-hour hard paddle against the wind to Copper Mine Dam. Ryder had been right. This must be an Alberta Clipper. He'd survived some bad storms, but he'd never been on the river during an Alberta Clipper. Damn Brand! What a fool! He may look like Matt, but the similarity ended there. Nobody in their right mind should be out here. He kept checking the shoreline to see if Brand had given up and might be hiding along the riverbank.

The water was blacker than he had ever seen it except where the fierce wind produced white froth-tipped waves. It was almost impossible to gain headway. Judging from the height of the waves heading into him, it was hard to believe he was going downstream. Intently watching the river's motion, he couldn't help but wonder what it was like beneath the surface in a storm like this, probably calmer than above, but there had to be a hell of an undertow. Many times, when throwing a lure downstream, he'd tried to imagine what was going on below that magical surface. Casting upstream never produced much action. Were the fish facing upstream tonight as usual waiting for some delicacy to float downstream like when he could see them on a clear day with the sun overhead? Or were they hidden below some protective rock patiently waiting out the storm? Convinced fish knew more about storms and barometric pressure than he did, Weston had learned how they fed voraciously when air pressure was low before a storm and then laid low for days after weather disturbances.

So how in hell did he get himself in this mess—out in a Clipper chasing a stupid escapee. But he knew why. He'd go to any length just to see Brand back at maximum.

SEVEN

CARL WESTON, SUPERINTENDENT of the Northwood Correctional Prison, had tapped his foot anxiously awaiting the newcomer, Jeffrey Brand. He should be at a sectional meeting, but Wednesday was arrivals, and he'd never missed a new prisoner arriving at camp. He could size them up right off the bat.

He stared at the bold print across the top of the paper on his desk, "Process and Indoctrination," and leaned back in his swivel chair. Shape 'em up, keep 'em in line, forget the bold print. Weston smiled. Scare the hell out of them was more like it. Folding his arms across his bull chest, he felt a sense of pride. He performed his job well but not from any prison manual and certainly not from the new prison revisions.

Pure experience, he trusted it. Forget the written crap. For the past thirty-five years he'd knocked the rebellion out of prisoners that needed it, and most did.

Rules had slackened of late but not with his approval. He had given a little here and there, but if he'd learned anything in all these years it was to stick to the old ways that worked.

Reading Jeffrey Brand's dossier, Weston noticed nothing special. Listed as a native American-Indian, Brand seemed like another smart-ass inner city kid gone awry with drugs and armed robbery. Suddenly, Weston noticed a special problem—rape attacks from prison inmates. That would never go on record in his prison.

His office smelled stuffy, and he leaned across his desk to push open the lower window. A cool breeze defied mid-summer. It was still crisp as early June. He gazed over the grounds, admiring his territory, proud of the well-kept buildings, the bright green lawn, a pristine look beneath the mid-morning sun. Prisoners were either out with the Bull Gang, in school behind the main building or at assigned jobs. It was peaceful.

Tall white pines outlined the curved entrance drive, and Weston's eyes traced it to the narrow bridge crossing the Eau Claire River at the prison entrance. The rivers were his mainstay, his guidance, kept him centered.

No sign of the van, and he checked his watch. Not late yet. He could always count on Ryder to be on schedule. Good man.

North of the bridge the river slowed and widened into a small lake. Near the water's edge, the lawn ended abruptly where tangled alder bushes and cattails took over. Behind a stand of birch trees, a crew of prisoners replaced rotting boards in a fishing dock along the riverbank. Long ago, Weston had approved fishing privileges for the prisoners during off-time.

Hell, Weston thought, the kid's going to think he's come to some country club.

Beyond the lake, the Eau Claire River narrowed. Escaping over rocks and sandbars, it carved its way downstream. Dividing the town of Northwood from its cemetery, the river joined ranks with the St. Croix River a few miles below, forfeiting its identity. Weston grew up on tales of these rivers when Indians, trappers and French explorers had used the waterway for centuries as a passage between Lake Superior and the Mississippi River. The biggest deal they had reported was the formidable black flies. That hadn't changed.

The St. Croix and Eau Claire rivers claimed separate sources.

The Eau Claire took its form spewed from a lake. Then fed by bubbling mouths of underground springs, it gathered force on its way to an unnamed immortality. To Weston's eye nothing had changed since his boyhood except the white pines were taller, so tall, in fact, that an evergreen canopy thwarted the undergrowth, padding his feet with pine needles. As long as Weston could remember, the Eau Claire had nourished him, brought him to his knees reaping its harvest of trout and muskrat. In spring, watercress choked crevasses along the bank. He could count on that.

Long ago, his father homesteaded this land along the Eau Claire after arriving destitute with a wife and child from Canada. His mother always claimed her arms grew two inches longer from carrying river water up the steep bank to their cabin. After marrying against his mother's wishes, Weston and his Indian wife, Maria, raised their boy and girl at the same place on the Eau Claire in much the same way as he'd been reared. Abandoning the Eau Claire was unthinkable.

Before it swallowed the Eau Claire, the St. Croix River claimed its source from deep within a primeval forest, seeping its way through loamy earth before gaining strength to absorb the Eau Claire and emerge as the tributary Weston revered. He always thought these rivers' opposing origins were a paradox. The St. Croix had emerged as a virginal spring before turning into a watery gathering place, while the Eau Claire emerged from a chain of lakes to become a brief thirty-five mile trout stream fed by pure cold water springs whose fate was to be dissolved by the grand St. Croix River. Gathering force the St. Croix frothed its way downstream, draining Northwestern Wisconsin as it acquired lesser streams, nobly shoving aside everything in its determined wake to join the race to immortality, only to lose its identity to the Mississippi River two hundred miles downstream. On the other hand, it eased his mind to think maybe the St. Croix hadn't destroyed itself after all, only changed its name. The St. Croix deserved to live on forever.

Weston relaxed in his swivel chair, propped his feet on the desk and looked at his wall of awards, all proof of his excellent record at the Northwood Prison Camp. There had been no revolts. There had been a few escapes, but none had occurred in the last twenty years. All had been captured. Twenty-five years of success. Nothing could destroy that. Two more years, and it would be behind him. He'd live a normal life, travel, fish, hunt. All there waiting—still, it would be nice to have another rehabilitation under his belt. Here at minimum, the end of the prisoners' line, odds for a successful rehab were supposed to increase.

Not that his own life had been all that easy. There were times after Maria died when everyone converged on him. "Get out," he'd told Maria's Indian cousin when she'd wanted the children. "You're too busy," she'd countered. But he knew it was because he wasn't Indian. Maybe no one else knew it, but he'd loved Maria, and he loved their kids even more.

Her Chippewa family never understood him. Once a year they would gather to harvest wild rice on a marshy lake east of town. Weston never figured out where he stood in that ritual. By nature of their birth, native Indians held the rights to harvest wild rice fields. Non-Indians had to petition for permits to participate.

Each canoe was apportioned a section. Everyone started at the same time, swathing their way through the swampy crop. Poling back and forth, they gleaned the ripened grain from rice stalks. Weston always felt guilty claiming a tract to harvest just because Maria was in his canoe. Perhaps he should have put in with the "outsiders" for his permit, especially since he didn't hang around for the week-long celebration.

According to tradition, the rice was harvested in one day. He missed that part now remembering how he stood in the stern pushing the canoe forward through tall stalks of grain. Maria sat in the bow facing him with two slim sticks, rhythmically sweeping the reeds across the gunnel of the canoe with one hand then swiping the grain from its stalks to the floor of the canoe with the other. Weston was proud of her. It wasn't quite the way the Indians did it, though. Traditionally, the man stood in the bow with a pole pulling the canoe forward while the woman sat in the stern gathering the rice. But this way he could watch her, called it her rice dance.

He would lose himself with just the two of them hidden within the tall stalks as rice gathered at their feet, slowly growing to their ankles and mounding to the calves of their legs. The effect was soft and pleasant. He could barely see over the top of the reeds, but once they made the last turn in their apportioned swath in the rice field, he lost interest. After that, for his blood, too many people were out of control.

For the next several days, these Native Americans feasted on what Weston called food, ritual and chaos. Fires were built while the men stomped on the grain with new moccasins to thresh the rice from its hull. Next the grain was dried and cured over fires. They no longer needed him. Happy to leave his Indian family to their heritage, he returned to work. Now, his daughter Evie wanted to cling to their ways, determined to find her guiding Indian spirit, and it worried him. He was afraid he would lose her.

In the early 1800's there had been an Indian village on the St. Croix above a beaver dam. The natural dam created a sizable body of water and swampy wetland called Whitefish Lake where wild rice flourished and was harvested by the Chippewas. Weston always wondered if Maria had been a descendant of that clan called the Fish Clan. No one seemed to know. He'd never talked about it, but he might ask Evie if she knew about Chief Kabamappa, the leader in that village. From what Weston was told as a boy, the story did not have a happy ending. On second thought, he didn't want to encourage this Indian Spirit obsession she'd been following lately, too afraid it involved finding her dead brother's spirit.

Once again Weston searched the drive for the van that would deliver the new prisoner.

No fences or guns contained the seventy-five men at the facility. Wilderness alone accomplished that. Wise to its ways, Weston saw the forest as freedom in its purest form, but every prison official knew why only criminals from the cities were sent to Northwood. Prisoners built their own prisons with the bricks and mortar of nightly howls and screams from wild animals. Few entertained thoughts of escape.

Periodically, there were a couple lifers at the correctional facility, mostly murderers that had eventually cycled their way through the system to minimum. They were model prisoners destined to carry the weight of their sentences, knowing they would never leave prison. *Carry the body,* they called it.

Then there were those who couldn't quite leave the fold. How ironic, Weston thought, a system geared to rehabilitate men back to a society that generated repeats simply because the machinery had done too good a job reforming them, making them so dependent they could never exist outside the system. Most of the prisoners were on their way out, though, knowing minimum was the last stop, hoping to make it on the outside.

It pleased Weston how smoothly his regime worked. Nothing much changed from day to day. He was proud of that. Before they knew it, they'd be back at maximum if they didn't follow the rules. Every five years the Wisconsin State Correctional system rewarded Weston as a model superintendent because he commanded the respect of both camp guards and prisoners. He smiled looking from plaque to plaque lining his office wall that documented his success.

EIGHT

THE UNMARKED PRISON VAN slid past city limits leaving
the Milwaukee maximum security prison in its exhaust.
Civilization disappeared. There one minute, gone the next.
God knows, he wanted to be transferred away from the sexual
assault, leave maximum security for minimum. He'd be an idiot
not to want that. Everybody wanted minimum—the last stop
before going back to the bricks. Jeffrey Brand, city boy, pretty
boy, knew he'd been tagged, knew that's why the parole officer
had arranged the stint at minimum despite the five years left to
complete his sentence.

Never out of the city, Brand knew its ways. He had learned
to creep through its bowels to survive. Like a stray cat, he distrusted whatever looked safe. Before incarceration for armed
robbery, he'd always escaped from what had become his curse,
his prettiness. Girls liked him a lot, that was okay, but so did the
prison studs. Half Indian, tall and lithe with long black hair,
he'd become the perfect make.

Buildings disappeared. Except for a few small towns, open
fields and farmhouses transformed into wilderness.

"Where the hell is this Northwood?" he asked the correctional officers in the front seat.

"Nowhere you've ever been, Mr. Brand," one of the officers answered.

"Shit," he muttered. He hadn't counted on this. "I didn't know they put prisons in the woods. How much farther?"

"A few hours."

Unable to sleep, he grew more and more agitated as huge trees and thick forest vegetation encroached upon the highway.

"Any wild animals?"

"You bet."

The most he'd ever dealt with was a ferocious dog. "Like what?" he asked.

"Oh, raccoons, deer, skunk, coyotes, wolves."

"Wolves! You kiddin'?"

"You'll see."

The only wildlife he could remember seeing was squirrels and maybe a rat or two along the Milwaukee River. Once he'd gone to a zoo with his school hoping to see wild animals but came away disappointed. Caged animals didn't count. Avoiding the side window, he settled back and stared straight ahead at the highway.

Suddenly the guard slammed on the brakes, and Brand lurched forward.

"Chrissake!" he screamed.

Directly in front, a huge black bear ambled across the highway. The animal was fearless, even stopped and turned to face them with defiant composure.

"Shit," Brand leaned forward, "I never seen a bear before. That's a real bear, for Chrissake. Get the fuck out of here!"

The guard laughed. "You're in for a treat."

"I don't believe the shit you kick."

Throwing back his head, the guard driving the van laughed raucously, then turned serious. "Watch your language, Mr. Brand. You won't get away with that up here. Superintendent Weston is a man with strict principles. He gets respect."

"You just playin' me out?" Brand said, leaning back with a smirk.

"We have a non-believer here, Mr. Ryder," the second guard said. "Need to see it to believe? That it, Brand?"

"Okay, okay," Brand muttered.

"Come on, come on, move out, fella, no free rides," Ryder joked, turning the van out and around the bear as it meandered off and disappeared in the woods. "We've got plenty more bears at camp."

"You betcha,'" the guard added, "right out at the garbage dump."

Brand slouched into the corner. Minimum was sounding more like maximum.

NINE

CHECKING HIS WATCH, Weston was relieved to see the van pull in right on time and rose to greet his newest inmate.

Jeffrey Brand stepped from the vehicle flanked by the two guards.

Weston groaned. A pretty boy. He pumped his jaw muscles watching the young man slump up the front walk. No one stood up straight anymore.

As the prisoner neared the entrance, Weston stared. Something about the young man was strangely familiar. The eyes. The long black hair. The slight build. Weston winced. Wanting to turn away, he held his stance. Weston nodded first to the new prisoner, then to the guards to pass.

Instead of following them into receiving, Weston slipped into his office and dropped into his swivel chair. What in hell was going on, he wondered. The very sight of Brand angered him.

"Mr. Weston," Ryder said, poking his head into the room. "The introduction tour."

"Yeah, sure."

"You going to do it?"

"Of course." Weston rose and followed Ryder into the receiving room.

Dressed in street clothes, Brand was the only new prisoner. His boxed belongings on the table served as a prop for his elbow as he slumped, legs sprawled, tapping his feet.

"On your feet, Brand," Weston said roughly, looking him over. Good-looking, Weston thought, slight, but handsome. He hated the relaxed dress code they had to follow these days that put him on the same level as the prisoners. Until recently, all correctional officers wore tan uniforms, and prisoners wore green uniforms that were a distinctly different style. Now, except for a badge on his utility belt, he looked no different than the inmates. He'd liked the confined feeling of being in uniform, stiff tan shirt, razor creased pants, spit-shined shoes. It had defined his role, separated him from the inmates. It was a clear message of who was boss and in control.

One thing Weston refused to relinquish was his well-starched look, making sure his shirt and pants were always pressed. Relentlessly, he wrote state officials pushing for officers and prisoners to return to uniforms, but the prisoners had won. 'That's just the way it is' speech is what they'd given him when he countered with his lack of respect argument. Inmates wore what they wanted, and it made him mad as hell to think about it. They could choose the green pants and shirt uniform issued upon arrival or wear their own clothes. Few opted for the uniform. Weston had no choice but to wear street pants and shirt.

Brand refused to move. Weston grabbed Brand by the shirt front and jerked him to his feet.

"We have rules here," Weston growled.

When Weston released him, Brand collapsed into the chair.

Angry with this upstart, Weston grabbed his shirt again and twisted the front of his shirt to squeeze Brand's throat as he pulled him to his feet.

"You're lucky there's no 'hole' here—the 'hole' is back at maximum. Remember that."

Ryder moved forward to stand between Brand and Weston.

"Well, Mr. Brand, this is your last stop on your way to reform," Weston began, collecting himself, then had to look away.

Those eyes, dark Indian eyes, wary yet all-knowing. He hated to admit they could mesmerize him. His son, Matt, had had those same deep brown eyes that looked right into a man.

Weston cleared his throat and began again. "While you're here you'll do just that," he said, "complete your reform. My name's Superintendent Weston. You will call me that. This is Mr. Ryder. You will call him that."

The urge to look down was so powerful he had to force himself to lock in on the inmate's face.

Narrowing his eyes in confrontation, Weston continued, "If you behave yourself, show respect, take your work seriously, you'll get along here. Follow me. We'll take you around."

Once again Brand hesitated.

Brand had arrived in the van with belly chain, his hands attached to it. Ryder had removed the restraint when Brand stepped from the van.

Pointing to the chains, Weston said, "You won't get stripped on arrival here either, no de-lousing shower, no routine bend over and 'stretch em' search. You've probably been naked for more cops than girlfriends."

Weston resisted a smile and waited as Ryder guided Brand to his feet. Weston led the way.

They proceeded through a door leading down a long corridor, looking into prisoners' rooms along the way. The rooms had two cots and two foot lockers.

"These are the doubles. A few singles down the first hall. We house seventy-five men here."

Brand shuffled his feet along the floor with each step.

"Pick up your feet, Mr. Brand."

In the old days, he would have issued conduct points for such behavior. He shook his head knowing he couldn't do that today.

Weston stopped in front of a door that opened into a small cubicle of a room. "Here's your pad. All the essentials—your locker, wash basin. Toilet's down the hall. Leave your gear on the bed, Brand. Mr. Ryder will show you where to find what you need later. Laundry, mess hall, rec and TV room, toilets, all that. He'll introduce you to your roommate. Who's in here with him, Mr. Ryder?"

"Dollar Bill," Ryder answered.

"Thought I'd be alone," Brand said.

"You have to earn that," Weston barked.

Weston had reservations about the combination. Dollar Bill was too cool, but Weston needed him. A natural leader, Dollar Bill kept a semblance of order. All the same, no need to teach this renegade any new tricks.

"Here are the out buildings." Weston was irritated by Brand's blank stare. They pushed through the heavy door that led outside.

"Nice day," Weston said, and they all looked up at the cloud-free sky. "Should feel good to you up here—being in the north woods," he said baiting Brand. "Paradise. Smell those pines. Nothing like it."

Weston watched the effect it had on Brand as fear crept across the city boy's face. At least he'd come to attention. A flock of crows flushed from the top of White Pine reminding Weston of crow shooting with Matt. They were a tricky target, but Matt had a good eye.

"See you *almost* finished high school," Weston said and led him into a building that housed a school room and the library.

Once inside the annex Brand looked too comfortable to suit Weston as though he might flop into a chair and put up his feet.

"Mr. Jack's the boss here." Weston pointed to a balding heavyset man helping a prisoner at a computer. Another inmate was busy at a desk working from an open book.

"You need to finish your education," Weston said.

Brand shrugged and eyeballed the prisoner working at the computer.

"Here's the machine shop," Weston said once outside.

"I done that back at maximum."

Even Brand's voice made Weston's son flash to mind, and it bothered him. Every minute of every hour, Weston steeled himself not to think about Matt. Now here was this loser that looked too much like Matt. They could have been brothers.

Weston directed Brand across the grass to a large garage. "The men learn welding here. There are plenty of jobs to choose from. A lot of the men sign up with the Bull Gang to work out in the forest."

"Don't know about that," Brand said.

Who did this smart-ass kid think he was, anyway, telling the superintendent he'd think about it like he was choosing a college course. Weston looked to Ryder who remained stone-faced.

They walked Brand back to the main building in silence. It was lunchtime. Prisoners were lining up for noon chow.

"I'll show you where to wash up, and you can catch up in line," Ryder told Brand.

Weston headed for his office.

Back at his desk, Weston opened a folder his secretary Sue had left him. It was next week's schedule. State officials would arrive next Tuesday for a prison evaluation. No problem. He'd press the officials to tighten regulations such as going back to uniforms. He would mention Brand and explain how a uniform could correct his attitude. He shoved the calendar aside, unable to concentrate.

Ryder popped his head into Weston's office. "You okay, Chief?"

"Sure, why?"

"I never saw you react to an inmate like that before."

Weston rose pounding one fist into the other, angrier than ever when he thought how Matt's life had been snatched and here was this half-Indian trouble maker, probably never having done a thing right in his life. It infuriated him.

"Never mind, Ryder. I'll manage."

TEN

"HEY, YOU!" A PRISONER yelled from one end of the mess hall.

Brand looked up from his plate. The heckler along with other men at the table laughed. Brand looked away. Same desperate men, Brand thought, same buggy, beady, squinty eyes, heads too big, too small, men too big or too small. Bold tatoos of skulls, women, demons and snakes, all staring him down. What else did he expect? A guard stood at the mess hall entrance. The guards did seem different, though, more relaxed, no uniforms, he liked that. But the inmates all smelled of distrust, same as maximum. The fear was always there. Kindness was a weakness—recklessness respected and admired. Eye contact was to threaten. He would still have to fight for his safety despite being at minimum.

"They won't bother you none so long's you don't back off," the man sitting next to him said.

"What do you know?" Brand snarled.

"You know what shit they kickin,' Brother?"

Brand shook his head in disgust. He'd keep up his guard.

"That stands for A U, stupid, Ass Up."

"Think I don't know that?"

"Forget it, brother. Anyway, we gonna call you Curly from

now on, on account of all that straight hair you got. Chow down. The grub ain't bad today."

Brand slouched down to his food, but he hadn't much taste for macaroni and cheese. He hadn't thought the inmates would be so tough on him, but he should have known. Why would he think anything else after all the shit he'd taken.

"Yer in the best restaurant in town, so like I told ya, chow down. Besides yer roomin' with me. You got lucky." He slapped Brand on the back.

Brand finished eating in silence while the man babbled on. He knew when to retreat into himself.

"Name's Dollar Bill. We gonna get along real good."

Dollar Bill stood up and yelled across the room to the heckler. "Shut up, Lucky. Curly here don't like that shit."

Brand frowned.

"Hey, Curly, I'm gonna' save you. You'll see."

He couldn't figure this dude.

"What's going on in here?" Ryder said, poking his head in the mess hall from the galley. "Someone looking for a conduct report?"

The men quieted as apple pie ala mode was served on the counter.

"Get back to business," Ryder warned. "Ten minutes until afternoon shift starts."

Brand cased Ryder. He noticed Ryder had a way with the men, how they shut right up when Ryder spoke.

Brand fell in behind Dollar Bill and the other inmates lumbering along as they left the mess hall. At least he wouldn't have to endure the twelve to fourteen hour sleeping jags like when he'd first entered maximum, a stage all new felons went through, he'd learned.

Out in the hallway, Ryder stopped Brand. "Meet me in the reception room. We need to work out your schedule."

Brand made his way as quickly as possible to meet Ryder. He wanted to distance himself from the others. Play it cool. He'd have to ride it out with the inmates.

"Here's our program," Ryder said, sitting across from him at one of the tables.

Brand studied the paper. "So?" he finally said.

"See anything here that interests you?"

"I never been asked that before."

"I don't believe that," Ryder said. "Do you like basketball? Gardening?"

Brand guffawed. Back at maximum, there were no options.

"Okay, let's get serious. You have choices here. We have a baseball team."

"Baseball? I dig baseball." He'd hardly played baseball in his whole life. Who'd have him on their team, a loser like him.

"Sounds good, our team plays local towns around here. Show up after five o'clock chow across from the front entrance." Ryder scratched his head. "Now for your work job. What's your experience?"

"Nothin,'" he paused, "that counts." He thought of asking if they needed someone to heist a truck.

Ryder shifted through his papers. "You don't have to decide today. I could put you on the Bull Gang that works in the forest. There's a space. Get you outside."

Brand couldn't believe he'd drawn that wild card. He'd seen enough of the woods on the way up here. "Anything else?" Brand asked.

"Interested in getting your high school diploma?"

"Sure," Brand answered. Anything'd be better than the wild woods.

"I'll see if Mr. Jack can fit you in."

"Mr. Jack?"

"GED teacher, you met him out back."

"To do what?"

"We'll see, especially if you're going to work on your diploma."

Brand didn't know what to think. "Sounds like kindergarten."

"Go unpack your stuff. I'll meet you at Jack's in fifteen minutes. Remember where to go?"

Brand nodded. He wasn't used to so many choices.

Dollar Bill was on his cot in their room when Brand entered.

"Hey, Man, what shit they give you?"

"School. And the library, I guess."

Dollar Bill doubled over with laughter. "Library? What the fuck you gonna' do in a library?"

"Catalogue or categorize they told me. How the hell do I know?"

"You know how to read, Curly?"

"Course I can read, any dumb fuck can read."

"Go with it. Take the fucking order. It's a sweet job. Hell, it can't be all that bad."

Brand turned away. He'd better not offend this dude especially since he was his roommate. "And baseball," Brand said, calming down.

"Well, ain't that prophetic, Curly one." Dollar Bill stood up and coiled himself over Brand's bunk.

Brand eyed Dollar Bill's position on the bed, leery of the pose.

Dollar Bill continued, "I just happen to be your star pitcher. Maybe you'll shine as my catcher. Hang in there, Bro. See I told ya I was gonna save ya."

Brand headed for the toilet. He didn't know what to think. Was this another make on him? He needed that like he needed another . . . he couldn't find the word and pounded his fists against the door.

By the time he found his way to Mr. Jack's annex, Ryder was waiting for him.

Ryder nodded to Mr. Jack when Brand appeared, and Brand sat down opposite.

"Let's see what we have here," Ryder said, opening Brand's

file. "You have another year's work to get your diploma. You could shorten it, I bet."

Brand looked toward Mr. Jack who nodded.

"Want to go for it?" Ryder asked.

"Might as well," Brand said. He didn't feel one way or the other. He'd need to clear out of the prison during the day, anyway. Just a gut feeling, but he sure as hell felt safer out here in the annex. He'd never spent much time in a classroom and looked around at the tables and books. Yeah, might be okay.

"Let's get started," Jack said. "Ever use a computer?"

Brand stared at the machine and started to laugh. "You kiddin? I hardly ever seen one let alone touch one."

"You're going to do more than touch one, Mr. Brand. You're going to learn to use one."

"Hmm," Brand eyed it. This could be cool. He'd heard about the internet, but had no idea how to get there.

"Come in here." Mr. Jack walked into an adjacent section of the annex. Books lined the walls. "The men come three days a week to read and check out books. Like to read?"

Brand had always liked to read, just never had much chance. "Sure," he said, then turned toward Ryder. Maybe he was getting in too deep.

"I'm going to give you a test now, and we'll see where we go from here." Mr. Jack pulled out a chair for him.

Brand looked around for Ryder, but he'd left.

"Uh, Mr. Jack, I'm not sure . . ."

After the test, Brand walked along the book shelves. He spotted a book about edible wild plants and leafed through it. Might as well learn something in case they sent him into the woods. He figured the Indians up here probably lived off the land. Might come in handy someday, like if he decided to take off. As if he could think about escaping and wasn't sure what had made him think about it now. He still had five years to serve. Maybe it was the extra freedom he felt up here at minimum.

ELEVEN

WHEN BRAND RETURNED to his room, Dollar Bill had followed him.

"Did you pass, brother?" Dollar Bill laughed.

"Pass what?"

"They test all the new fish."

"Step off," Brand said. He wasn't going to let this creep get the better of him.

"I says to myself, there go an easy mark right there when I first seen you, Curly."

Brand thrust his fist in Dollar Bill's face, ready to punch him.

"Well, maybe not," Dollar Bill said and backed off. "We got a little time before supper. Let's go toss a few. We got a game coming up in a couple a days."

Some other players were throwing balls around the baseball diamond when Brand and Dollar Bill arrived.

"Don't say nothin,'" Dollar Bill whispered. "Just step behind the plate, and I'll toss in a few."

The others joined in, and they started a pick-up game. When it came Brand's turn to bat, he belted one over Dollar Bill's head. Brand couldn't believe he'd done that but decided to run like hell.

"Hey, you okay!" someone yelled from left field. "You knocked the shit out a' that."

"Those baby arms got SOME muscle—you okay, Curly!" Dollar Bill called to him.

Brand was so surprised, he could barely run and laughed himself to the ground as he slid into home plate.

By the time the game against the town of Northwood took place, Brand felt as comfortable catching for Dollar Bill as at bat. Ryder loaded the team in a van, and they headed for town. It was the first time Brand had been off prison camp grounds since he arrived. His stint on the Bull Gang hadn't started yet. The windows were wide open, and wind blew through his hair. He felt high. The last time he'd felt this good was right after the couple of joints and snorts before he got busted. He never dreamed something like riding in a car with the windows open could make him feel so alive. He watched the shallow river curl and ripple alongside the road. He wanted the ride never to end. The first thing he'd do when he hit the bricks was heist a car and ride around with the windows open.

The town proved closer than he'd thought and a lot smaller. All he spotted was a couple of houses, a tavern, and a post office. Once they turned off the main street, a lane led to a school, and the baseball field was behind that.

"Where'd all these motherfuckers come from?" Brand asked looking around at the crowd.

"Out of the woods, they is wood ticks," Dollar Bill laughed. "These wood ticks, they really into baseball up here."

Brand had never seen anything like it. They were cheering up a storm, and the game hadn't even started. Suddenly he spotted a girl staring at him. Part Indian, just like him. So pretty. Their eyes locked, and she smiled boldly. It's a miracle, he thought. He ached to talk to her. Maybe if he played real good, she'd say hi. Not in the rules. He'd been told about that before they got into the van. Ryder had made it clear. One mistake, and that was it—back to the wall.

Brand settled in behind home plate. Northwood had won the toss and was at bat first. Brand was nervous about dropping the ball. Dollar Bill threw the ball sharply inside. The batter took a home run swing and missed. Brand snapped the ball into his mitt with authority, then tossed it back to Dollar Bill, hoping the girl had seen that move. The game had begun.

After a couple of innings, he looked around the crowd wondering what brought them to watch a bunch of fucking losers. The Northwood team was beating up on them. Brand kept sneaking looks at the girl. She was always looking his way, smiling. Seemed she didn't mind if they were losing. Making sure Ryder wasn't watching, Brand winked at her while he waited his turn at bat. She held up a piece of paper. What the fuck was this? The hair on the back of his neck tingled.

By the fourth inning Brand felt like he was ready for the major leagues. He'd played pretty well, got on base twice and hadn't dropped the ball yet.

Everyone stood up halfway through the seventh inning. He'd seen the girl walk toward the bench. Then from behind, someone thrust a note in his hand. He looked over, but whoever it was, had disappeared. Too scared to look, he shoved the paper in his pocket.

He couldn't find the girl in the stands after that. No one scored on the prison team from then on, but he'd gotten on base one more time and only dropped one pitch from Dollar Bill.

The smell of hotdogs and mustard floated past Brand. He's never wanted a hotdog more in his whole life, but Ryder had them in tow going back to the van.

"Smell them dogs?" Brand asked Dollar Bill.

"Turn off your smeller, Curly."

Ryder had parked near the entrance so they wouldn't walk through the vacant lot where the towns people had parked.

Once back on the van, Brand asked, "How many times do we play Northwood?"

"Depends," Ryder said. "Some years we play Northwood a lot, depends on how many towns we line up."

"When do we play them next"

"They're coming to the prison camp next week."

"How about all the people?"

"Some of them show up."

Brand scanned the parking area looking for the girl but couldn't spot her.

Turning to the inmates now loaded in the back of the van, Ryder said, "Nice show."

No one said a word.

"What the fuck?" Dollar Bill finally said.

Ryder hadn't started the engine. "Did you try to lose?"

"We played like shit."

"That's not what counts. Not the score—well, what do you want to hear from me?" Ryder yelled. "Do you want me to give you a sucker to make it all right? Practice harder."

Dollar Bill laughed, his guffaws growing louder until the others joined in, doubled over in uncontrolled laughter.

"What's so funny?" Ryder asked with a smile and headed back toward camp.

Back at prison, Brand wondered where he could be alone to read the note. He went out to the annex. Jack had already left, and it was locked. He pulled the paper from his pocket and leaned against the back of the building.

It jumped out at him: "I love you. Come to church on Sunday. E." The words might have been written in red letters.

He hugged the note close. No one had ever said that to him. Love? Him? That's what people said on TV. He had to see her again, find out what she meant. Where was this fucking church?

What's this shit, Brand thought, spotting Dollar Bill splayed on his bed as he entered his room. Brand ignored him.

"You done good, Curly."

"So what? Get your ass off my bed."

"You tender vittles. Hey, that's some 'do' you got there," and gave Brand's long hair a quick flip.

"Shit! You fag," Brand snarled and grabbed a change of clothes.

"Hey, watch it, Curly, I got a stripe."

"Who gives a fucking shit!"

"Careful," Dollar Bill hissed as he slid onto the floor and slowly rose to his feet.

Brand slammed his fist into Dollar Bill's gut.

Dollar Bill coughed, grabbing his middle.

"I might accidentally miss your pitches," Brand spit into Dollar Bill's face.

"Yeah?"

"Step off!" Brand warned and pretended to slam him again in the gut as Dollar Bill retreated.

Brand headed for the receiving room bulletin board to look for a notice about a church service. He couldn't believe he was actually checking out a church but found it near the bottom: Lutheran Church Service, 11:00 A.M., Sunday. Van leaves from front circle 10:45 A.M. the second and fourth Sunday of each month. Sign here if interested.

He didn't even know if it was the right church. He didn't have a pencil, but it was only Wednesday. There must be just one church, he decided, or she would have said which one. Plenty of time to think about it.

TWELVE

CARL WESTON NESTLED INTO the first pew and beamed ear to ear as his Evie, dressed in a white choir robe, walked down the aisle of the Northwood Lutheran Church. Positioning himself front center, he faced his precious daughter. Pride for his sole surviving child consumed him. What a beauty, she looked just like her brother, same dark eyes. He loved her soft brown skin and black hair pulled straight back and up into a pony tail. The main reason he came to church every Sunday was to gaze upon and savor his offspring, his own flesh and blood standing before him in white. Despite the choir's supporting effort, her pure soprano voice alone filled the sanctuary.

Evie looked so angelic, it was hard to believe that this morning they'd had another row.

"I'm going whether you like it or not," she'd said.

Evie was still on this strange kick of finding her long lost Indian spirit. At first, he'd thought it a good thing, honoring her mother and her brother. Then she came up with this Resurgence of Spirit idea. Pure crap, start to finish, convinced it was a cult. One day last week, Evie said she knew her brother would return. Weston had laughed, but secretly it scared the hell out of him.

"His spirit is *too* alive," she'd said, as she turned her back on him.

Just this morning this Resurgence of Spirit thing came up again at breakfast. "It's a cult," he said. "A dangerous group."

"I'm not listening to you," Evie said. "We're meeting tonight at Mary Ann's house, and I'm going no matter what you say. You can't stop me."

"Where did you hear about all this? I never said you could commune with dead spirits."

"Mother did—listen," and she chanted meaningless words.

"What are you saying?"

"It's not the words, it's the sound. Can't you hear it? The sounds connect me to the past, and it's not dead spirits, it's spirits of the past."

"I don't want you going to any more of those spirit meetings. I can't get a grip on what this Indian spirit thing means."

"That's all you ever think about," she screamed, "getting a grip on something."

He couldn't take any more and slammed the back door on his way to feed the Precious. After forking in new hay and pouring oats in the deer's pan, he gave her fresh water. Weston lingered in the barn watching her position and reposition herself to and fro to secure her surroundings. She moved left then right lifting and circling her head in all directions. It fascinated him. He used to pity her blindness. Of late, he thought she actually found comfort in being blind. She had a constant protective nest, and he never saw her show alarm. But the doe knew nothing else, no romping through the woods.

Even though he dealt with it daily, out here with Precious, Weston realized more than ever the reality of confinement. He wanted to free her, but knew it would signal her death.

Animals in the wild had it tough. Weston took his chances in a world that didn't care for him anymore than anything else.

Precious looked content. He wondered if animals suffered mental anguish. Did Precious long to escape and run wild with a buck? Matt had always wanted to put a sign on her stall: The Buck Stops Here.

He wondered if Precious heard him close the kitchen door and crunch his way through the pine needles, knowing he was coming to her on schedule. Would she be disappointed to hear the cough of his truck engine as it resisted starting and then the rough rattle of the truck as it disappeared down the road? Could she imagine him plop into his swivel chair?

Order took a lot of work. Given all the chaos in the world, experience had taught him order was the only sane way. He scratched Precious on the neck as she leaned into him.

A train racing through Northwood pierced the barn with its urgency to arrive somewhere on time. How strange time was, Weston thought. Time took a breather out here in the stall with Precious.

Then Evie had opened the back door and yelled across the yard, "You're not God, you know, no matter what you think."

Not God, maybe, Weston thought, but I'm still in charge, and he repositioned himself to get comfortable in the wooden pew.

That spirit club Evie insisted on was wrong. Talking to her brother was nonsense. Christ, he'd been dead almost three years. He had to admit, though, Matt still came with him when he fished or hunted—sometimes up there on his shoulder just like when he was a little kid, and they talked—when no one was around. But then again, hard as he tried, he couldn't always conjure up Matt when he needed him. All the same, he didn't need any spiritual nuts to help him commune with his son.

Evie had gone on to say the unthinkable, "Besides, you killed him!"

"What did you say?"

"He played chicken."

Fire burned in Weston's face. Playing chicken meant taking a risk when the odds were against you—like lying on a railroad track in front of an oncoming train. Matt would never do that just because someone might call him "chicken."

"Why do you get so mad when you hear the truth?" Evie asked.

"I know the truth, and that's *not* the truth. It was an accident!"

"You wouldn't let him do *anything*. Just like you don't let me do *anything!*"

More than anything, Weston had wanted to stop quarreling and tend to Precious.

"Go feed your precious prisoner," Evie screamed at him.

He shook his head. The last thing he needed was another prisoner.

He concentrated on Evie's singing. Who'd ever think such wild thoughts could run through that pretty mind. Purity in her voice cut through his anxiety. He hadn't lost control of her yet, but he was afraid to think what he would do if he lost her. He couldn't even stand to think about after she would finish high school, not daring to imagine her going to college, let alone falling in love with someone and getting married.

He'd never considered remarrying after his wife's death. Oh, he'd looked at a few women. Debby, who tended bar at the Buckhorn, had invited him to her place several times. It became a joke. "When hell freezes over, will you come to my place?" she'd asked loud enough for everyone to hear so now he wasn't at all sure she meant it. Besides, he continually battled his prostate problem. He wasn't about to reveal that to anyone.

Maybe when Evie was all grown, he'd think about some companionship. For now he had Precious and the river and Evie. That was enough for any upright man.

Evie's eyes focused far over his head, beyond him, toward the back of the church. Couldn't she see him sitting here all alone, loving her beyond belief?

Weston read the order of service in hand and had to smile at the sermon title—*"Fish Catches Record Man."* This might be pretty good after all, he thought, unless it was some catch and release plan. That was for the summer swells. He'd always been a meat fisherman himself, keeping only what he needed. He had suspected the pastor was a bit liberal and wouldn't be surprised if he was one of those tree huggers—what with his trendy second-day beard. Probably a Democrat besides.

THIRTEEN

T HE HYMN ENDED, AND Pastor Holmquist walked to the lectern. "Good Morning." Weston could tell he expected the congregation to respond so he mumbled his "Good Morning" along with the rest.

"You may be wondering about the sermon title," he began. "My little joke—today's sermon actually concerns Jonah and the Whale. In a nutshell, Jonah was about the most prideful man to be found in the Bible. It seemed God went to Jonah, a Jew, and asked him to go to the town of Nineveh where there was rampant sin and warn them that God was going to destroy them unless they changed their ways. No way was Jonah going to help these Ninevites. He hated them. Instead he hopped on a boat going in the opposite direction as far from Nineveh as he could get, a place where he thought God did not rule."

Weston struggled to listen to the Bible scripture. Pride, that was the message. "Hubris," the pastor called it. He called it a sin. That didn't make sense. How could you hold your head up unless you took pride in yourself, Weston wondered. Pride in performance—that's what it was all about, and—it took courage—the warfare of living.

He looked around for people he knew who might benefit from this sermon, like Nels Anderson, for instance, who never said a wrong thing in his life.

Frankly, Weston was disappointed. He'd thought he might pick up a good fish story this morning, maybe something they could hash over at the Buckhorn Tavern. Maybe a record Muskie had flipped some guy's boat. God knows there were mammoth Northern Pike around just waiting for the taking. Trouble was no one at the Buckhorn was much into the Bible.

The pastor continued, "Once Jonah was on board, a horrible storm ensued. Jonah worried that it was God's punishment for failing to do as God had directed. He as much as told the sailors this, but as the storm worsened, the sailors would hear none of it and continued to fight their way through the tempest. Still the winds increased, and the waters whipped even higher. So the captain went to Jonah who was asleep in a bunk below. 'Maybe you were right, maybe it is your fault,' said the captain. 'The storm is worsening.' Jonah agreed and volunteered to be thrown overboard. Immediately, the waters calmed as Jonah descended into the deep where a whale was waiting to swallow him. Jonah lived three days and nights in the whale's belly."

Weston hadn't heard this tale in years.

"Jonah cried out to God for his salvation, and the Bible tells us Jonah said, 'But I with the voice of praise will sacrifice to thee: I will pay whatsoever I have vowed for my salvation to the Lord.' The Lord then spoke to the fish, and it vomited Jonah upon dry land."

The pastor paused for a sip of water. Weston checked his watch.

"Jonah then walked to Ninevah, but instead of loudly proclaiming God's message to reform, Jonah was so repulsed by these people and angry at God for bothering to save them that he walked around merely whispering God's message. No one heard him except for one person, and that individual told the king they needed to mend their ways, or Ninevah would be destroyed. The king responded, shaped up everybody, and God did not destroy Ninevah. Now this made Jonah so mad that he stomped out of town and sat under a tree and sulked. God proceeded to wilt the tree so that Jonah received the worst sunburn of his life, blisters and all.

"Still Jonah questioned God. 'Why are the Ninevites so important?' he asks. God never answers Jonah.

"My friends, Jonah sold his soul, but for what? Certainly not for his image.

We know how he did it. Look at Jonah's history. From start to finish he was hard-hearted and too full of pride. No humility. Why the whale? Jonah was swallowed by what? His pride, folks. That's what consumed Jonah!

I'm not sure Jonah knew why he traded his soul for what the return might be. He never got beyond his false pride."

These Bible stories might mean something to some people, Weston thought, but not to him and once again he looked around. Where was Mamie Anderson who ran the Fourth of July events with an iron hand, or Earl Peterson who lorded it over who should receive which cemetery plots? Not here, that's for sure. Why were sermons always directed toward the missing souls?

Weston had to admit he was curious about the idea of selling one's soul for a better image. His wall of awards came to mind, but he certainly hadn't sold his soul for any image on his wall.

"However," the pastor went on, "Jonah was not the only defiant, prideful character in the Bible. Don't forget Job. He also questioned God as to what was going on when God took away his wealth, family and health. And remember, my friends, Job refused to take any of the blame."

Weston checked his watch again, thinking please—no more pride.

"As opposed to Job who ultimately exhibited compassion for his friends who wrongly advised him," Pastor Holmquist said shaking his head, "Jonah, however, never looked beyond himself. At the end of the story, Jonah was left holding the bag, defiantly questioning the higher order of God. We aren't told what happened to Jonah. For all we know he remains forever seated beneath that wilted tree in the desert doomed to burn from the heat of excessive pride, longing for a cloudy day to heal his parched skin."

The pastor was really into this pride thing, alternately wringing his hands and gripping the podium for dear life, but Weston couldn't find the point. Jonah wasn't too smart in his book. Punish the wicked, that was it, and Weston knew all about that. If not, his last thirty-five years had been a waste.

"In conclusion, it is not the external events that make the man," the pastor said. "Opinion too settled in the mind becomes a permanent background."

Hogwash, Weston thought. He'd knocked that out of a lot of men. Christ, that's what his job was all about.

"Man can live anywhere he chooses," the pastor said, "even in the stomach of a whale. Man places himself. God bless you and Amen."

Weston's back hurt. He squirmed in his seat during the collection, relaxing only as the organ heralded the choir's departure. Evie seemed intent on another mission as she swept up the aisle, but the smile on her face was enough to make his day.

Jeffrey Brand had brought up the rear following Ryder and two other inmates who had signed up for Sunday church. Brand chose to sit on the aisle at the opposite end of the pew from Ryder in case the half-breed girl was there and passed close to him.

Organ music resounded from above and behind him. Trunk of bullshit, he thought, looking around the small white chapel. Everything was white, even the altar. Bunch of clampetts in here, goody-two-shoes. Hell, what did he know, he'd never been inside a church before, let alone one painted all white. Never thought he'd find himself sitting in a white church for any one let alone a girl whose name he didn't even know.

Then he spotted her in the choir, and right then he knew he'd never seen a girl like this before. Not a real one and a half-Indian like me. He could tell she had Indian blood. When the choir sang, her voice rose above the others. Excited as a tom finding a cat in heat, he broke into a sweat and didn't hear one word the minister said, just the rhythmic rise and fall of his voice like a bulldozer filling a dump truck scoop after scoop. Before long, Brand had his fill. Turning this way and that on the hard bench, he could hardly wait until this crap ended.

When the sermon was finally over, she walked up the aisle directly toward him. He couldn't breathe. She slipped him a note so fast he didn't see her do it. Just the smell of her so close by made him dizzy. Stuffing it in his pocket, he pulled out a kleenex for cover and blew his nose. He resisted looking to see if anyone noticed. When he turned to leave, Ryder and the other two had their backs to him and were walking out the aisle.

Ryder led the way to the van. "Get anything out of that sermon?" he asked.

No one spoke.

"How about you, Brand? What did you think?"

"I'm not into whales," Brand said, "but I liked the singing."

"Did anyone feel sorry for Jonah?" Ryder asked.

The inmates shrugged in unison.

"You men believe in God?"

They looked at each other and broke out in muffled laughter.

Once back at camp and alone, Brand read her note. She begged him to get on the Bull Gang so they could pass notes. He had no trouble on that score. He'd already received that sentence this past week. The Bull Gang didn't look so bad, after all.

FOURTEEN

"GET YOUR ASS IN THE VAN, Curly," Dollar Bill yelled at Brand who was lying on his cot.

Brand dragged himself to stand, and they walked together toward the van that would drive the baseball team to Northwood.

"What'sa matter, Man? You sick?" Dollar Bill asked.

"Shut up," Brand said as he climbed into the vehicle. He was tired, that's all. He'd never worked so hard, and every muscle ached. He'd signed on with the Bull Gang just like she'd asked. They'd been brushing a whole week at the State Park in Solon Springs, a few miles north of Northwood. He'd never seen so much undergrowth. They'd hardly made a dent. The undergrowth reproduced thicker than shit in Milwaukee. Nothing changed. One fucking clod produced another and another, and the girl hadn't shown up with any more notes. Who was she kidding? He'd let her know who was boss if she showed up at the game, let her know who she was messing with.

He'd written the girl a note to give her just in case she came to the game, and now he wished he hadn't. The note said he was working on the Bull Gang but didn't know where he'd be each day. He'd simply ignore her if she showed up.

Sure enough, there she was, and he couldn't stop himself

from winking at her, hoping she'd know he had a note for her. He watched her approach the bench, and as she pretended to fall into him from behind, he slipped her the scrap of paper. Before the game ended, she walked past again and handed him her reply. He dared not read it until he was alone, hoping she'd come up with some plan so they could meet.

Pumped to the hilt, he slammed two balls to the outfield and drove in two runs. The girl was all smiles. He hoped it wasn't because Northwood had defeated the prison camp again. They'd never won a game, not even come close, but he still liked base-ball a lot.

Her message told him she'd watch for the prison van to pass her driveway each morning and follow behind to see where they would be working. She'd leave her note beneath a nearby rock with a pointed stone on top. He was to take the pointed stone and leave her a note in the same way and tell her when he was working next. Don't worry, she'd find it, she said, and that way, they could write without anyone knowing, but they had to be very careful.

He'd never had a girlfriend who wrote notes to him. He was just thankful he'd gone to school long enough to learn to read and write even if he hadn't graduated from eighth grade, let alone high school. Maybe he could get his GED if he stayed here long enough.

FIFTEEN

BRAND WAS GETTING USED TO being in the wild. He liked unearthing the pungent smell of mushrooms settled beneath a rotting log and wondering which ones were poisonous. He studied their shape and color to look up in the library. Some-times surprised deer shot off through the trees, gone in less than a second. Hard as he tried, he never could spot them again in the brush. So the morning they were assigned to paint the Northwood Town Hall, he was disappointed.

"Painting sucks," he said to Dollar Bill.

"Oh yeah? Wait'll you see what an artist I am."

They pulled up across from the Buckhorn Tavern, and Ryder led them into the Northwood Town Hall.

Paint cans and drop clothes were piled in the center of the large room. Brand looked overhead. "I ain't painting that fucking ceiling. Shit, I'm scared of heights."

"Me, too," Lucky said.

"Okay, men, we're supposed to paint the bathrooms and the kitchen, so stop whining," Ryder said.

Some ladies poked their head in the door. "I guess exercise class is cancelled."

Brand followed Ryder back to the bathroom to get started. He'd never painted anything except for 'Fuck You' and 'Shoot

Up' on sides of schools, never anything like a wall in a room. He was going to tell the others about that but figured he was in enough trouble already with Weston. It would be pretty funny, though, to cover the walls with filthy words. No better place, he thought.

They worked steadily for two hours before Ryder said they could have a break and took them out back of the building. The sun was out, and the men leaned against the building having a smoke. Brand tipped his head to catch the sun on his face. It felt good. Sometimes prison wasn't so bad.

They'd barely finished their smokes when Ryder herded them back in to finish the bathroom. He showed them how to paint window frames, how to cut in around the window.

"Hey, Curly," Dollar Bill said, "check this out," and he pointed to a nude he painted on the opaque glass. "See? I told you I could draw."

Ryder caught it before the paint had dried and made Dollar Bill wipe it off. Brand thought it looked quite nice there the way the light streamed through the two big breasts.

By mid-afternoon they had finished the work and Ryder told them to go out to the van. Brand followed Lucky who motioned him to cross the street toward the Buckhorn. "Come on," Lucky urged. "Been a long time since I was in a bar."

"What you going to do?" Brand asked.

"I gotta take a leak. They gotta let us pee."

Brand held the door of the tavern for Lucky to enter. He couldn't believe the video games lining the walls. "Look at all that gambling garbage. Too bad we ain't got no cabbage."

Brand almost made it inside when Ryder grabbed him by the collar.

"Get in the van. Where do you think you're going?"

"To the toilet," Lucky said.

"You spent all day in a bathroom. Remember, you painted it."

"You gonna give us a report?" Brand asked.

"I should. I'll have to think about it."

Brand knew the last thing he needed was another conduct report.

Later in the week, Brand decided to check out the river before night curfew when he had to be back in the building. The river fascinated him with its swirls that ferried leaves, logs and bird feathers at will. He didn't want to get in the water, but he liked being near it. The river gurgled at intervals as though there were a hidden bubbler beneath the surface. He sat on the bank and threw sticks and leaves in the water pretending he was watching a race. Most of the time the leaves ended up winning. The sun sank behind pines on the opposite shore. He sat in the shade and watched as slanted rays highlighted the ripples, turned them silver. He'd have to come back to this country some day. Geese honked their way in to a landing as they settled on the river for the night.

A rustle caught him off-guard. Suddenly, there was Dollar Bill, including Lucky, along with another creep coming up behind him, crouching, ready to pounce. They rushed him, threw him to the ground, and hiked up his buttocks.

"We gonna tie you up and do you, Curly."

Dollar Bill laughed uncontrollably as they ripped his pants exposing Brand's ass.

"Here we go! A U, Curly."

"Fuck you!" Brand screamed and kicked at Dollar Bill as hard as he could.

"Now you know what I been saving you for, Curly."

"Stop right there," a familiar voice roared.

They turned to face Superintendent Weston with Ryder alongside. Dollar Bill turned to run.

"You're going nowhere," Ryder said grabbing Dollar Bill by the neck.

"It's the wall," Weston yelled. "All three of you."

Dollar Bill crumpled.

"On your feet, Brand," Weston said. He leaned toward him and hissed, "You're lucky we caught onto this."

Brand had a room of his own now that Dollar Bill was back at maximum, but he knew it was only a matter of time. He was marked, even more now that Weston and Ryder had saved him. The others would be after him—the superintendent's pet snitch. He would be "snitch" to everyone. No one would stick up for him. He had to break out, but for the life of him, he couldn't figure out how to do it.

He despaired thinking about escape. Escape was on his mind all day, all night. Maybe he should just kill himself. That would fix all of them. Then the prison would be investigated, and there would be a shake up, maybe Weston would get fired. Things might even improve. Trouble was, he'd never know it.

Just as he thought all hope for escape was gone, the very next day the girl had left a plan under the rock. Wow, he couldn't believe it. Here he thought she'd given up on him. Maybe he could pull off an escape, after all.

At night he couldn't sleep, going over and over what he would do, step by step. Sometimes he thought it would work, but the next minute he was too scared. Then a second note came:

"You can do it. Here's how." She'd signed it simply "E," adding more minute directions.

SIXTEEN

BY THE TIME BRAND HEARD the roar of the rapids, it was
dark. Snow engulfed him. His arms ached from paddling
against the wind even though he was going downstream. These
rapids were wider, and he could tell they were a lot longer than
the last set. He chose to go with the swiftest water this time.
The current created a V at the head of the rapids. The canoe
glided easily down the middle of the V, but quickly the current
dispersed and it was anyone's guess where to go. Suddenly, he
found himself crosswise between two rocks. The canoe tipped in
an instant, and he was dumped into the water. He clung to the
canoe, just like the girl had told him. The water was warmer
than he'd expected. Despite the cold, it was much warmer than
the air. The canoe hadn't taken on much water, and luckily the
water wasn't too deep, just faster than hell. He pointed the bow
downstream and hopped back in the canoe. He was proud he'd
recovered, but the current immediately shoved him toward the
shore and scared the hell out of him. He found himself shooting
down the right side of the river, boulders to the left, shoreline to
his right. It was a huge drop. Crashing along out of control, he
came down hard on a boulder that didn't tip him over but made
him veer abruptly to one side, and then just as suddenly the
canoe dropped into a calm pool at the foot of the rapids. He

laughed like an idiot. He hadn't laughed that hard for a long time. Looking back upstream he marveled at the tumble of rocks and the violence of the river.

"I made it," he screamed to the sky as snow fell onto his tongue. Once as a kid, he'd lifted his face to the sky to feel snow on his tongue, but this tasted better than ice cream. He thought he might have been reborn in this dark water and emerged as a new person. He drifted along the shore savoring his new high.

Spotting a campsite sign, he stopped to pee and plowed his way through more than six inches of snow on the ground. This must have been someone's cabin, he thought. There was a distinct clearing, and it looked like special trees had been planted. He imagined a long-ago road now overgrown. What a spot. Back at the canoe, he rummaged through the plastic bag tied to the front of the canoe and found sandwiches the girl had made. Damn, he wished he'd asked her name. He couldn't believe how hungry he was once he started eating. He could have eaten the whole sackful but knew he had to save some for later. He wondered how this place looked in the summer. The evergreen trees were so big and strong; they must have been here forever. It was comforting to think something had been here before he was born and was still alive. He'd come back here someday and camp. Water hissed at him as it combed rocks along the shallow shoreline. He almost tipped over again as he stepped into the canoe, but managed to steady it. Once seated, he shoved off into the wind.

He'd been paddling for what seemed like hours. He touched his head. Protruding from his hat was a crown of frozen hair. The wind had to be 35 miles per hour or more. Maybe there were no more rapids, and he could find his way with no trouble. He tried to remember the maps of the river he'd studied and thought he'd memorized. But by now he was confused, and nothing was like he'd imagined.

The snow fell harder. If only it would stop or ease up, the going would be a lot easier. The force of the wind blocked out all other sounds. Except for the wind, everything was muffled. He kept telling himself there was nothing to be scared of.

Once he passed the next bridge, he would look to the left for a river joining the St. Croix, and then he would head south, hoping it was the Yellow River, but from what he remembered from the river maps, the Yellow River was several hours ahead, especially against this wind. He would stop once he'd headed up the Yellow River and would figure out how he could camp for a couple of weeks, find food in the forest. He wasn't sure what faced him ahead on the river, but at least he'd gotten this far.

Thank God the temperature hadn't dropped drastically. As long as he paddled at a steady pace, he kept warm despite being wet. The foul weather gear contained his body heat.

Ugliness of the past summer angered him. He'd expected it would be better at minimum and was disappointed. The superintendent hated him for some reason he couldn't figure. Dollar Bill had closed in on him. He'd been pegged as a snitch. But the girl was a plus, and baseball had been great. Much as he hated the Bull Gang work, it had made him stronger, and he'd gotten used to the wilderness. Still, he couldn't figure the superintendent. Brand knew he didn't have much of a chance at the prison having been labeled a "make" *and* a snitch, but for the life of him, he couldn't figure out why the Big Man was out to get him. He wasn't worried about what would happen if he got caught—after all, he was the victim. He'd get himself a lawyer.

His arms felt like they were going to drop off. The aching had turned to numbness, but he could take it. He was tough. He figured he'd been in this stretch about two hours. It would be a boring part of the river in normal weather, straight forward with few curves, a few ripples now and then. But tonight, it was unbearable against the wind and snow. If only he could look for edible plants or peer into the forest.

Stroke after stroke, he paddled on, pleased he managed to paddle the canoe in a straight line now. He had definitely improved. It was as though he'd learned how to do this in some former life. Shitty as the weather was, he was at home on the river in this strange wilderness.

Sheets of snow pelted him dead on. Suddenly a structure loomed in front of the canoe. The bow spun right and swamped in the trough of a huge wave. The canoe crashed up, then down. Water poured into it. With no time to think he was swept between two boulders and straight down a shoot. The canoe hit hard, and that was the last he knew until he woke up floating downstream buoyed by his rain suit, no canoe. He shook his head to clear his brain. The cold helped. Frantically, he tried to gain his footing by back stepping, pushing his legs against the bottom until he finally stabilized himself on the slippery gravel. He must have been knocked out, he figured. His head hurt. At first, he couldn't breathe, but then after a few moments and deep breaths, he began to slide his feet along the slippery rocks toward the shore. He figured the boat had caught along the shoreline at some point downstream. So now all he had to do was get to shore and feel his way along until he spotted it. Simple enough. This was definitely not in the plan, but he could handle it.

Alder bushes laden with snow hung heavy over the edge of the boggy shore, bobbing up and down. He hoped he was following the side of the river where the canoe might have hung up on a snag. He crept along beneath the scraggly undergrowth, feeling his way. He could barely make out the opposite shore but kept looking across for signs of the craft. Shoreline brush helped protect him from the force of the whirlwind-driven snow. The water was not deep, but his head still ached from being thrown into the river. He must have hit something. "Shit," he muttered as he spit blood into the water. Things had been going well up to now. It had been scary but fun. Now all he had to do was find that fucking canoe with his belongings secured in the bow. Too bad he'd eaten all the grub. He grabbed at roots or whatever was strong enough so he could pull himself along. If only it would stop snowing so he could see where he was going.

Not sure how much time had passed, he stopped for a breather. This was taking forever. He crept along the shoreline. No sight of the canoe. What if it had snagged on the opposite side of the river? What the hell—daylight would come eventually—then he would find it. No one in their right mind would try to capture him tonight.

A howl made him jump. What would be out in this fucking weather, and he stopped for a moment, clinging to the base of an alder bush, listening, looking around him. He couldn't see a thing. Maybe it was just the wind. What could animals do in this weather, anyway? Nothing, if they were smart. Maybe he wasn't being smart. He must start thinking like an animal, maybe hole up somewhere safe until it was light. He could always find his canoe hung up along the river when it got light, and the storm was over.

He looked into the woods for a fallen tree that could serve as a cave. He'd seen a TV survival movie where some guy had made it for weeks living under a fallen tree. Continuing to feel his way along the bank, he crept through the water, grasping at whatever the shore had to offer. He wondered where that eagle was in all this—hiding or maybe enjoying this slop.

Suddenly, his feet went out from under him, and he fell backwards. One hand grabbed the bank while the other found the river's rocky bottom just as something thrashed at his legs. "Yeow," he yelled as a fish sailed upward through the water landing smack in front of him. He fell backward. It was huge. He'd never seen a fish that big. It must have been hiding along the shore. He'd better get on land fast. He scrambled to his feet, now running both hands along the shoreline, grasping at spindly trees and boggy clumps, searching for a good spot to slide out of the water. Once on land, he could crawl inland and find a fallen tree or bush to shelter him. Suddenly, something clamped onto his forearm.

"AAAHHHGGG!" he screamed. Teeth dug into his flesh. Pain jolted him backward. A bear, he thought.

Then he saw the steel trap latched onto his forearm. He jerked to free himself, embedding the iron jaws further into his flesh. Its teeth pierced his clothing and sank into his arm. He'd heard a crack and thought his arm had broken. It hurt like hell. He felt faint—had to get out of this cold water. Crawling further onto the bank, he strained to worm his body out of the wetness, inching toward a snow-laden cedar bent close to the ground. There was still some slack in the chain. Sliding beneath the branch, he pulled the chain along that secured the trap. He found himself in a snow cave. Pain stabbed throughout his body. He'd never known such agony. Rolling into a ball, he rocked back and forth moaning and alternating between cries and screams.

He lay this way for what seemed like days, in and out of consciousness between frightening dreams of horror. When conscious, he was scared that some animal would crawl in with him, into his snowy cave, thinking it was safe as he had. Here he was—a fucking prisoner again—in a white prison, trapped like some fucking animal.

If only it was daylight, maybe then he could think of a plan to free himself. The longer he lay there, the more convinced he was that he was going to die. He knew he hadn't died and gone to hell—it was too cold. He'd never really thought about death, not his own anyway. He'd seen a couple of guys get shot, but not killed. Sometimes he wondered if his mother was dead. It might be better if she was, then he could stop hating her for leaving him on the streets and feel sorry for her because she was dead. He couldn't even remember what she looked like. Was she the Indian or was his father? Maybe they both were, but he thought she was the Indian.

Maybe someone would find him after all. It would be better to be captured, taken back to that fucking prison, back to the wall, back to Dollar Bill again, whatever. Maybe when it got light, someone would come looking for him—maybe the girl would tell someone he escaped on the river—maybe they'd find his canoe.

Who would miss him anyway? No fucking mother that he knew—maybe the girl would miss him. She'd made him promise to come back. He was afraid of being eaten alive. He imagined animals descending, smelling his death, before he was even dead. The Jonah sermon raced through his mind. Jonah almost died in the whale, but he never gave up hope. He couldn't believe he was remembering a fucking sermon.

It was still snowing mountains, he could tell. But under the tree, protected from the wind, everything was quiet, all noise silenced by snow. Even his screaming was deadened. The world was deaf to his agony. Nothing could hear his pain. He'd surrendered his body and his voice.

Thank god his arm was numb now. He packed more snow on it with his free hand. It didn't hurt so much all frozen like this. It *would* have to be his right arm. He would have to be fucking right-handed. He was getting sleepy and knew he couldn't stay awake much longer. It must be almost daybreak. Who could tell what time it was in this fucking snow storm? He didn't have enough energy to get mad. Maybe if he took a little nap, it would be light when he woke up. Instinctively, he knew he shouldn't sleep, and he tried to imagine his girl bending over him, kissing him all over.

What the fuck was wrong with him? She'd gotten him into this. It was all her fault. If she hadn't encouraged him, he'd be back at the prison, safe, waiting out his term, staying out of trouble.

It was horrible not knowing if night had become day or maybe he'd slept, and day had turned into night again. Everything had turned inside out.

He dropped into a dream wrapped in pain. Hidden enemies in the woods were circling, advancing, wrapping so tightly it hurt, and he woke to intense pain. He was going to die, and he was going to let it happen.

Intense shivering and dread made him wonder if he was dead because he couldn't feel the cold. Something was hunting him. He listened to the endless stamping of trees marching to the wind like drummers gone crazy in some parade. Someone once took him to a parade. Was it his mother? He felt so alone in this swirling world of snow mounding above him. He was in his grave. The fiercer the storm became, the quieter it seemed. It was almost cozy if only the pain would lessen.

He pulled his legs into a fetal position, and screamed. Aside from the pain, he cried because he knew a scream would never be heard. He'd grown weary of the endless night in his sound proof cave. What if he cut off his arm? He had no knife. What did animals do? He'd heard they chewed off their arms or legs. He didn't have the energy.

He welcomed drifting into a stupor, and before he knew it he was back at prison.

Saturday night had not been Brand's favorite. The library annex was closed. After staring out the window at the end of the long narrow hall, he wandered down to the TV room. Except for a couple dozen plastic folding chairs and a small TV hung from the ceiling by a metal frame, the white-walled room was bare. There were no windows. He slouched into one of the chairs scattered about the room and pulled over another to prop up his feet.

The prison had no cable or satellite connection, just rabbit ears for reception, bent where frustrated inmates had tried to find better reception. It was a snowy picture at best. You had to be pretty bored to watch this crap, Brand thought. The first station offered a cooking show. Shit, he didn't even like to eat, let alone cook. It occurred to him that he'd never lived where he'd had good food to eat. Prison slop was crap. Before that, he often stole food. He switched channels to a baseball game that wouldn't lock in and kept rolling from the bottom to the top of the screen only to reappear after the play had finished. He was too lazy to stand on a chair and find the vertical control button to adjust it, so he sat and watched whatever flashed on the screen. The prisons around Milwaukee and even the jails had better reception than this and much nicer TV rooms. The tougher the prison, the better the recreational facilities, he decided. Leisure time at minimum stunk.

He noticed that Lucky had been up to his tricks again. The first time he'd seen the creative display in the mess hall it made him sick, but now he had to smile. Lucky fashioned fake turds out of wet toilet paper using dirt to dye them brown and left them in absurd places for all to admire. One was cleverly placed and blended into the brown folding chair next to him as though it lived there.

He was thinking of leaving when Lucky sauntered into the room. He'd never forget that Lucky was the one who'd bugged him the first day he arrived. He slid one foot after the other across the floor like Groucho Marx walking on stage. Brand ignored him. Lucky grabbed the chair Brand was using to prop up his feet.

"You blind or something'?" Brand said. "What's wrong with the other twenty chairs in here?"

"Watch what you say, snitch."

Brand jumped to his feet and grabbed Lucky by the front of his shirt, pulling him within an inch of his face. "Nobody calls me 'snitch.'"

"Snitch, hanging out with Weston, we're on to you," Lucky spit back.

"Motherfucker," Brand yelled in his face. He grabbed Lucky's hair with his free hand and slammed it against the back of the chair. The chair collapsed. "You're fucking lucky, Lucky, that chair was plastic." Brand dragged him toward the wall. He was determined to beat his brains out just as Ryder ran into the room.

"Hold it." Ryder grabbed Brand by the arm. "Get yourself to the infirmary, Lucky," and shoved him toward the door. "I'll see you in my office later."

Ryder wrestled Brand into a chair and stood before him. "What's gotten into you? Now I have no choice, Brand. This makes your third conduct report." He waited for Brand to defend himself. "Why?" Ryder asked.

"Nobody calls me 'snitch.'"

"That's not a good enough reason to try and kill a man."

Brand looked away.

"Still living in the moment, aren't you? When are you going to learn to think ahead, like the consequences? Some things just aren't worth it, Brand. Something else going on? Come on, what is it? Why did he call you a snitch?"

"Is that all, Mr. Ryder?"

Ryder shook his head. "That's all, Mr. Brand."

Brand walked from the room thinking a fourth conduct report was only a matter of time. Being a snitch was a death sentence. Escape was looking a lot better than going back to maximum.

"Have a seat," Weston said as Brand entered his office, trying to downplay his growing irritation with him.

"Something wrong?" Brand asked, fidgeting in the chair.

"How's school going? They tell me you like to read."

"It's okay."

"I've heard reports about you. Just wanted you to know. Want to hear it from you."

"I'm okay," Brand muttered and looked away.

"What do you mean 'okay'?" Weston raised his voice. "You've got three conduct reports for fighting. Why?"

Brand stared out the window.

"Look at me," Weston said. "You're safe here, no one can hear you."

"I ain't no snitch," he snarled.

"No one said you were. Use your head, Brand."

Brand tapped his foot. "That all, Mr. Weston?"

"Not quite. What books are you reading?"

"Anything."

"Jack says you've been reading about nature."

"I hate nature, scares the shit out of me."

Weston could have slapped another conduct report on him for insolent language, Brand thought. He couldn't do that for such a slight offense as bad attitude, but Weston was relentless when it came to control.

"So why the sudden interest in nature?" Weston repeated.

"Some weirdo wrote a book about eating wild plants. Couldn't believe anyone's that crazy. I got a cousin who works in a natural food factory. He don't eat that crap, though. Says he'll find me a job when I get out."

Again Weston ignored the language. "That's enough."

Brand made a disgusted face.

Weston rose making direct eye contact with Brand. Brand rose to meet his gaze without lowering his eyes.

"That'll be all for now, Mr. Brand." Weston gestured toward the door. "Your attitude could stand improvement, Mr. Brand."

"What the fuck?" Brand had said defiantly when he read his work order. "What's this shit!" He walked into the guards' office next to receiving and threw the paper on Ryder's desk.

"That's correct," Ryder said, reading the report.

"Fuck," Brand muttered. "Double fuck, triple fuck," and he beat his fist against the wall.

"Enough!" Ryder commanded. "It's still good weather. You'll

be the better for it. You can still work on your GED. Don't forget you're packing three conduct reports."

Fucking luck! Nothing was going right, Brand thought. Besides, the girl hadn't shown up at the last baseball game at the prison. He'd played real good, too, and she hadn't even been there to see him get two of their three runs. So what if they hadn't won. Ryder said it just mattered if they tried. He'd tried his damnedest. So where in hell was the girl.

"Hear you got the Bull Gang," Dollar Bill smirked.

"What the fuck? You got a hot line hookup?"

"You hangin' out with the Big Man too much. We don't cotton to no snitch."

"I ain't no snitch. Get out of my face."

Things were crazy around here. He headed for the annex, grabbed the book on edible plants and sat down to read. At least he's been able to look for plants out in the woods. Some of the commonest plants were edible, like cattails. He'd seen a bunch of them tails down by the fishing pier.

Brand woke with a start. The dream depressed him, and he wondered why he kept rerunning dead information. His arm throbbed like crazy. He managed to grab some snow with his left hand and pack it onto his arm. With each scoop, he moaned, louder, then louder. If only he could cut his arm off. Right now he would gladly die. Fuck the crappy world. He'd be better off dead.

He hoped the river was satisfied. He moaned in unison with the trees as their branches complained, rubbing against each other producing a weird muffled music that wailed with each gust of wind. The music made him think of the strange stuff his cousin liked, the one he'd told the Superintendent about and who said he would give him a job. His cousin didn't have a natural foods factory, but once he had said, a long time ago before he went to jail, "Call me if you want a job." He guessed that was his mom's relative. He looked Indian. He'd met him in a bar. Maybe he wasn't even his cousin, but he'd come up to him, said he recognized him, and thought they were related. The music that night had been weird like what he heard in the forest, more of a scraping whine than a tune. He'd never seen the guy again, but he did leave him a phone number, long since lost.

Sinking deeper into depression, he quieted, and then he heard it—splashing. He held his breath. It must be a bear, he thought, it had to be to make that much noise. He stopped moaning and waited. Maybe whatever it was would pass by him. No animal could smell death in this cold and wind. But there was blood. He'd bled all over the god-dam place. Animals smelled blood from anywhere. Maybe there were wolves here. He imagined them circling. He'd heard them howling at the prison garbage pit. He'd rather be shot than eaten alive. He was very awake, and the more awake he was, the more often the pain came, wave after wave with stabbing throbs.

He screamed to no one, "Fuck the world!"

Maybe he would scare off whatever it was. If he fell asleep now, maybe he would freeze to death. Then he'd never give a shit who ate him. Maybe some fisherman or a bear would smell him rotting in the spring thaw and finish him off morsel by morsel. What about when the man who'd set the trap came to check out his catch. Will he ever get the surprise of his fucking life. A dead Indian—some trophy—maybe stuff it and hang it on the wall.

He stopped thinking to listen again. The thrashing sound moved closer. Then he heard heavy breathing. Undergrowth was being brushed aside. He thought he saw a light. Maybe he was delirious. Pain convulsed him again. He groaned.

SEVENTEEN

A s Weston approached Copper Mine Dam, snow descended with a vengeance. It was well after mid-night, hopefully close to daybreak. He felt for his watch. Why in hell had he forgotten to put on his watch? He never went anywhere without his watch. In fact, he never took it off. He'd taken it off for some dumb reason back at the house. Now he remembered. The toilet was plugged, and he'd removed his watch to use the plunger. Dumb idea. The watch was waterproof.

He could hardly see through the onslaught of snow where to enter the sluice dam. There were hidden pilings that could be seen only in bright sunlight. He couldn't risk it and at the last minute decided to portage, steering the canoe sharply to the left shore. Struggling, he pulled the canoe up and over the steep embankment, slipping and sliding backwards before he was able to skid down the other side on the portage path, past the small campsite and reenter the river.

The campsite triggered a longing for his son, Matt. It had been a good spot to stop for lunch while fishing the river. Matt loved it. As a little guy he'd jumped from rock to rock in the shallow rapids. Once a big Northern Pike grabbed the worm on the end of his fishing pole and pulled him down flat on his face. He clung to the pole, and struggling to stand he reeled in the fish while tears streamed down his face. When he grew bigger he learned how to bump down the sluice dam without getting hurt.

Weston planned to spend some time searching below the dam to determine if Brand had gotten into trouble at the sluice dam. He would scour the south shore for a couple hundred yards before paddling upstream to Copper Mine Dam to check out the north shore. This would be the most likely place to find Brand in trouble, but then he may have made it through by some miracle. Or he may have tipped over and drowned, floating on down the St. Croix until some snag caught him. Weston had to admit he wouldn't mind that outcome.

He decided if he didn't find Brand between Copper Mine Dam and Steel Bridge, he would give up the chase and stop at the fishing cabin, thinking maybe Brand had taken to the roads and not the river after all or maybe had drowned. The snow was so deep now, no one could get through to wait for him at Steel Bridge. Below the bridge was the fishing shack, accessible only by the river, that he'd used for years. He could stay there until the storm let up. One never knew what an Alberta Clipper had in store. So what if he didn't find Brand. Was Brand worth risking his life? He'd done his part in the search. Not long ago, he'd overheard himself called "Old Weston." Go ask "Old Weston," they'd said. Was he really too old for all this? Then why wasn't anyone else at the camp up to this capture—who else had volunteered—had the stamina, not to mention the knowledge, to survive the St. Croix in an Alberta Clipper.

Deep down, he knew he couldn't give up the chase and simply paddle on down the river. He'd never been a quitter, even if Brand was a loser. Poking along, he examined every indentation in the bank, but there was no sign of any life along the shore. Normally, he would have found animal tracks, mud slides or trampled growth. Nothing, all was hidden beneath the snow. He moved cautiously, afraid of missing some sign of disturbance. Snow continued to fall, furiously at times, then subsiding into what he considered a damned heavy snowfall. Trees were so burdened they drooped to the water, threatening to break, and he had to duck way down to make his way beneath the canopy.

The river was shallow and wide along this stretch. It was hard pushing the canoe along the rocks against the current. He resisted getting out to shove or pull the canoe along, but a couple of times he had to step out when the canoe hung up on the shallow bottom. He shined his flashlight ahead and then to the side into the wooded shoreline. Trees and undergrowth were so thick, it would be impossible to walk on shore even without snow. Finally, when he flashed his light downstream, he saw Steel Bridge in the distance. He scanned the opposite shore and thought he saw something that flared in his light. He paddled cross current toward it, and sure enough, it was a canoe. Heart pounding like crazy, he was not sure what he would find. Maybe Brand was asleep or dead in the bottom of the canoe, or waiting to shoot him. He could have easily stolen a gun along the way. He turned off his light as he crept toward the spot.

He slowed to sidle up silently. The wind was against him— that was a help. He felt for his gun, reassured to find it still resting against his hip. As he moved closer to the canoe, he couldn't see any sign of life. There was a bundle in the bow covered with snow, but it didn't look like a person. Pulling alongside, he recognized Clarence's canoe, empty except for a garbage bag that was secured to the gunnel near the bow. Now he knew for sure. A paddle lay toward the bow.

Weston stepped into the water to secure the wayward canoe. No need to drag it upstream with him now. He was certain Brand was somewhere between here and Copper Mine Dam, hidden or drowned.

Working his way toward the bow of Brand's canoe, Weston's feet flew out from under him as he stepped on a slippery slab of rock. The bottom was mostly gravel or small boulders, so the flat rock surprised him. He hit bottom with a thud. Righting himself, he regained his footing. There was no rope tied on the stray canoe's bow—that seemed odd. Returning to his canoe, he cut a length of rope to secure the stranded canoe to a tree along the bank. It was lodged so precariously between a rock, the bank and an alder bush, Weston was surprised it had hung up at that point, but the current was slower along that stretch. It would have slipped away on its own sooner or later.

Suddenly, Weston realized he hadn't checked in with Ryder for some time and grabbed for his cell phone. It was gone. He felt all around his waist. What the hell? He couldn't believe it. He thought back. Maybe he'd lost it portaging Copper Mine Dam. Maybe he'd lost it just now in his fall. He traced his way back feeling the bottom with his feet. Probably wouldn't work out here in the storm anyway. His flashlight was no help to see beneath the water's black surface. At best during daylight it was hard to see anything on the river's dark, sometimes boggy, bottom. He raged at Brand who'd forced him out here on a night like this. Nothing to do but go ahead. He could hardly wait until he caught the renegade. He'd teach him a thing or two. When the storm ended, he was convinced someone would find them. The problem was that no one knew about the fishing shack if he decided to stop there. Ryder wouldn't have a clue as to where the cabin was.

Securing Brand's boat, he climbed back in his canoe to maneuver upstream along the north shore. The water was swifter than when he was floating down the opposite shore. Brand had to be along here somewhere. He must have capsized at Copper Mine Dam. Weston had to give him credit for getting this far especially in such a ferocious storm. The wind was at his back now even though it was tough going upstream. If only the snow would let up, but he didn't hold out much hope, judging from past Clippers.

How many Al Clips had he known, anyway? In his sixty years in the north woods, probably a dozen, maybe more. Once, he and Matt had been caught by a storm while partridge hunting along the east shore of the St. Croix river north of where it absorbed the Eau Claire. Most men used dogs to hunt partridge or ruffed grouse, but Weston prided himself on being a quick shot and didn't need a dog to flush the birds. Matt was actually a better shot than he was. Shooting partridge was a challenge. You had to practically step on one before it would flush, but the birds had been skittish that day, confused, and they'd been able to shoot their limit. Weston hadn't sensed the coming storm, but apparently the birds had. It had been a tough hike up the bluff and along the river, so when the snow hit with a fury, they'd hightailed it back to their truck. Normally, he cleaned his birds in the field, saving only the breast portion, but there'd been no time. That Clipper was a humdinger. They made it back just in time to inch the truck along the snow-blocked road. He'd never forgotten when Maxine and Jack Lynch, owners of the grocery story in town, were caught in an Alberta Clipper and had to spend the night in their car. Almost frozen to death, they were found later the next day and lived to tell about that year's Clipper.

His eye caught a break in the shoreline. He pulled hard on his paddle to move closer to the shore but spotted nothing unusual. It turned out to be an area where an eddy had cut into the bank. He persisted against the current, inching his way along. What spirit this river had, continually tearing at its earthbound confines. Unrecognizable undergrowth hung in tangles over the water's edge. Even his flashlight couldn't penetrate the woods. Here and there a fern that hadn't died stood regally decked out in white, reminding him of Evie in her choir robe.

What would Brand be thinking, Weston wondered. After losing his canoe, where would he go? You'd think he'd wind his way along the bank to try and find his canoe. If he didn't find Brand along this shore, he'd have to cross over and scour the south shore again.

EIGHTEEN

WESTON WAS TIRING AND PLOPPED onto a snow-laden
alder bush to catch his breath, his feet dangling over the
edge of the river bank. He longed to be back at the Buckhorn
tossing a few with Ole. Poor Ole—his heart got him.

The Buckhorn Tavern had its regulars who lined the bar
watching whatever television had to offer. Not that Weston
counted himself a regular like some, but he felt comfortable here
beneath these furry quadrupeds fortifying the walls. He could
mingle with folks who didn't question who they were or what to
expect tomorrow. Life's surprises revealed themselves at the end
of a gun barrel or a fishing line. The Buckhorn was not a place
where folks went to get drunk or escape but to embrace conversation and tell tall tales—not unlike church, Weston thought.

He waved to Palmer, the owner, but didn't recognize anyone
from church. He was disappointed because he wanted to talk
about the pride sermon, maybe hear what Pete the plumber
had to say about selling one's soul for an image. He didn't
quite get it the way the pastor had laid it out, and he needed
to run it by someone. He couldn't find Pete who often went to
the Buckhorn after church, but did spot Les Peterson, normally
a regular churchgoer.

"Where were you today?" Weston asked. "Didn't see you in

church." Les shrugged and headed for the football betting board. Weston knew Mamie wouldn't surface. Her pious nature didn't include Sundays at the Buckhorn.

The special today was a buck muffin accompanied by the Packer zinger that featured a shot and beer chaser. Weston went for the buck muffin and the beer.

Ole Bergquist arrived, and Weston waved him over to the oilcloth covered table where he sat.

"Where have you been, Ole?" and he called to Palmer, "Another beer, Palmer."

Weston had never been happier to see anyone. Ole Bergquist knew everything Weston's father had skipped telling him whether about hunting, fishing or women.

Ole ambled over, eyeing the electronic machines lining the wall as though he might slip in a video game or two, but the football game was about to start. No one began a serious conversation until all bets were placed on the Green Bay Packers and posted on the wall behind the bar beside the mirror that reflected the customers. A twelve-point deer trophy was mounted alongside the betting board, its head cocked toward the board as though to ensure honesty.

"How's fishin'?" Weston asked.

Ole hemmed and hawed.

"No luck?" Weston asked. "Fall fishing's not the greatest."

Ole frowned and ran his hand back and forth over his bushy eyebrows, "Don't know where to begin."

"Uh—oh. Sorry I asked."

"It'll come out sooner than later, might as well tell you."

Weston thought Ole was about to stir his coffee with his thumb and handed him a spoon.

"Nothing went right from the start," Ole began. "Had to go back for an extra canoe paddle, then discovered I'd left behind some of my best lures. But I did have my favorite one-eyed hair frog. So I went ahead."

"I remember that moth-eaten excuse for a bait."

Ole broke into a smile. "That miserable frog caught more fish than you ever seen, Warden. Anyway, I was paddling down the St. Croix, got to the rapids at Elizabeth Island and decided to go down the right instead of left side of the island so's I could pop my bait in a special spot before hitting the main drop." He stopped to shake his head and mop his unruly eyebrows.

"Not enough water?"

"Naw, that wasn't the problem. Here's the embarrassing part. A beauty of a bass snapped up that ol' frog before it could hit the water—didn't I say it was irresistible? So I got all excited for Christ's sake, and the damn canoe flipped. That old bass saw his chance and clean broke the line."

"Give a lot to have seen that," Weston laughed. "Especially the dumping part."

"Plum fool, I was. Worst of it was he kept jumping right in front of the canoe and proceeded to pop up all around that eddy like he was being paid to perform. Made my old heart sick just to watch his shenanigans. You ever tip over in that spot, Warden?"

"Can't say I have, but it's a rough one when the river's full."

"Well, the story gets worse. That bass was out to get me—big time. I went on down the river after that, but I couldn't get that bugger out of my mind. I took out at Scott's bridge, lost my taste for fishing. Later that same night, Paul Klink came driving up to my place—acting kind of cocky and all. He held up this fish by the line, bait still hooked in its lip. Big grin on his face.

"'Recognize this?' he asked.

"I took a hard look and said, 'Don't reckon I do.'

"'Well,' he said. 'I think you were outsmarted this time, Ole. Take a good look at the lure.'

"I did a double-take. It was my one-eyed frog. 'Where'd you get this, Klink?'

"'Down where the river spreads out just before Scott's

rapids—all tangled in the weeds. Didn't happen to tip over, did you, Ole?"

"I stared down that fish, 'Taunt me, will you?' So I had to tell Klink the whole story. He laughed til I thought he'd piss or pass out. Then he hands me the fish, still laughing, and says, 'Here, it's yours.'"

"Did you take it?"

"Damn right I did—never deserved a catch more in my life, even if it hurt my pride."

Weston leaned back and laughed his head off.

"Ever hear anything the likes of it, Warden?"

"Can't say that I have, Ole. That's quite a fish story."

Weston thought of the sermon. Ole wasn't worried about protecting his image. He'd just turned it into a joke.

A commercial came on, and someone hit the mute. Weston overheard his name and looked toward a man seated at the end of the bar. He couldn't quite place him. Then he remembered. The guy had had a cousin in the prison a few years back, and he'd hassled Weston back then about mistreatment.

The man caught Weston looking at him. "How's everything out at play school, Warden? I hear you gone soft," he said elbowing his buddy. "Gone from abusing to babysitting, I hear."

Weston's face turned red, and he turned to watch the TV, ignoring the man. He knew there were those who hated him for his position of authority and wanted to piss him off.

"Come on, Warden, ain't you gonna defend yourself? See? What did I tell you—he's gone soft. An old man gone soft."

Weston rose, gave Ole a pat the back, "Don't worry about your image, Ole—it'll never be ruined in my eyes." Weston threw some change on the bar and waved to Palmer.

Walking directly past the heckler on his way out, Weston stared him in the eye and said, "Listen up, Mister, twenty years now, and there's never been an escape on my watch. I've been busy protecting your butt so you can sit here and suck on a beer."

NINETEEN

DRIVING HOME IN HIS TRUCK that day, he was annoyed to think he couldn't stay with Ole and watch Green Bay cream the Detroit Lions. All because of that smart ass. But then the world was loaded with jerks too full of themselves who thought they knew it all—that's what the sermon had been about.

He'd never forget that day last winter when a former neighbor put a dent in his truck while it was parked at the post office. Weston saw him do it from inside the post office. In fact, it looked intentional the way he'd backed into Weston's fender while turning around on the road—a wide road, at that. He drove off and when Weston confronted him, the man denied it. Then the slob had the nerve a month later to turn Weston in to the game warden for taking a road-kill deer home for his freezer instead of to the food pantry for the poor. Nobody respected authority anymore.

A car he didn't recognize was parked in his front yard. What was this all about? Then he remembered Evie was having a meeting at the house with her girlfriends.

"Dad? You're home so early."

"Kicked out of the Buckhorn."

He pulled up a chair and joined them. "Hi, girls, what's your meeting about?"

"You remember Ann Marie and Sherrie," she said introducing the group seated in a circle around the dining room table. "This is our Spirit Club I told you about."

"Can I sit and listen? I won't say anything."

The girls looked at each other, stifling giggles.

"Dad, please, it isn't funny. Our meetings are just for members."

"Guess that leaves me out." He rose from his chair eyeing the TV in the corner and sat down to watch the football game here and flicked on the channel.

"Dad, really," Evie rolled her eyes at her friends. "I haven't fed Precious, maybe you could . . ."

"Later. This is a big game. I got a number on the winning score at the Buckhorn."

"We'll go upstairs," Evie told her friends. "Thanks a lot, Dad," she said turning her back on him.

Ann Marie grabbed the Indian blanket they had spread on the table.

The thought of Evie's 'find your spirit club' or whatever she called it scared him. The other girls didn't even look Indian like Evie or Matt or Brand, for that matter. She'd said this spirit thing had to do with finding their Indian ancestors' spirit. Her mother had never been into that. He'd have to ask more about it because it didn't sit right with him.

When the game was over, he was disappointed that his bet didn't even come close to paying off. He hoped that bum who baited him in the Buckhorn hadn't won anything. He'd check it out with Ole, hoping Ole had cashed in.

At loose ends, he decided to go feed Precious.

Precious was predictable. She leaned toward him in her blind deer fashion for a serious scratch along the neck or wherever else he decided was a good spot.

Opening the top section of the barn door, he gazed through the pines onto the Eau Claire River. "I wish you could see this, poor blind Precious. The sun is slicing right through the forest spotlighting the ferns. The leaves are starting to turn, seems kind of early. Swamp maples are already bright red. I've got you beat on seeing, but I bet you smell it all, don't you?"

By the way her nostrils flared he figured she could tell a smell as subtle as the river's spray as it splashed skyward against a boulder apart from curling leaves or browning pine needles bedding down the forest. He'd bet on her knowing tree mold from fungus. "You've got me beat on hearing, too. I'd give anything to listen to just half of what you hear," he said as he scratched the back of her ears while she nuzzled him. Who knew what all she heard—probably way into the forest where a tiny mouse was disappearing under pine straw.

Weston noticed she always got a little antsy as fall approached. It was rutting season, but he'd not seen any bucks hanging around. He'd have to remember to close and latch the barn door. He spotted where she'd been kicking along the bottom of the door and had loosened a couple of boards since yesterday. "Not trying to escape, are you?" He found a couple of old boards and nailed them solidly across the bottom.

"We can't have anyone violating you."

TWENTY

EVIE HAD LED ANN MARIE and Sherrie to her room and slammed the door. "Stupid man!" she hissed.

Sherrie sat down on the bed, but Ann Marie motioned them to join her on the Indian blanket she'd spread on the floor.

"It's okay, Evie. We want to be on the floor anyway. I just learned about the woman's traditional sitting position when she is in the tent. Sit on your right foot and extend your left leg, not cross- legged like I thought. This way the woman could rise easily to reach things, and her left leg wouldn't get cramped."

"That is so neat!" Sherrie shouted. "We should learn one new thing about Indian women for each meeting."

"Shhh!" Evie slowly opened the bedroom door to listen.

"What's your problem?" Ann Marie asked.

"Shhh, I can't let my father hear. Okay, are you ready for this?" Evie lowered her voice.

"I guess."

"I saw him."

"Who?"

"It was at the baseball game, like, he was right there."

"Have you gone crazy? Who are you talking about?"

"This Indian guy came to bat. I swear it was Matt. Same eyes, same build, same hair."

"Well, sure, he'd have the same hair if he was Indian. What's the big deal?"

"I stared at him, like, who *is* this? *And,* he stared back at me."

"So? Plenty of guys stare at you." Ann Marie shifted from her Indian woman position. "You're gorgeous, as if you didn't know."

"Ann Marie, shut up!" Evie heard herself yelling but didn't care. "Do you want to hear what happened or not?" lowering her voice. "I thought we were in this Spirit club together."

"I want to hear," Sherrie said.

"I gave him this note at the game," Evie whispered. "I could tell he felt this . . ." Evie struggled to find the right word—"spiritual pull—just like I did."

"So what did you tell him—that he was your resurrected brother?"

"Ann Marie, I never said that!" Evie paused and looked past her friends. "I *said* I loved him. But, yes, he is my spiritual brother, connected to my brother Matt. He doesn't know it yet, but believe me, he is.'

"You said you loved him? You remind me of that dumb Suzie what's her name that helped some prisoner escape—boy, did she regret that."

Ann Marie moved close to Evie and took her hands. "Look, Evie, we never said this Resurgence of Spirit was about reincarnation, somebody reappearing as someone else. Get with it!"

"Then what is it about?" Evie asked.

Ann Marie looked to Sherrie. Sherrie shrugged. "I'm not sure."

"See?" Evie said. "I'm not saying that either—all I'm telling you is—I felt it, like, big time. I wasn't looking for this. It just happened."

"Did you talk to him?"

"No, I haven't ever talked to him. I just give him notes."

"Notes? How often have you seen him?"

"Just twice. I saw him again in church today. I had written him to come to church, and he did. I can't believe he came, and I felt the same thing again, that connection with Matt."

Ann Marie shook her head.

"Listen," Evie said as she leaned toward the girls, "Listen to this—I have to save him. Believe me. It's my mission. Nobody could save Matt when he died. I have to save this guy." She burst into tears. "He looks just like Matt," she blubbered.

"Okay, okay," Ann Marie said touching her forehead, her mouth and then the Indian blanket. "Let's say the pledge."

The girls put their arms around each other. "Nothing read, nothing said will ever leave this Indian bed."

After Evie calmed down, Ann Marie said, "Seriously, Evie, my folks will kill me if I get involved with a prisoner. What do you want us to do?"

Evie wiped her face with her hands. "Nothing. Just don't say anything to anyone, but let's please believe in the Indian spirit I've found."

"Your dad is going to blow a fuse when he finds out," Sherrie said.

"He won't find out," Evie said and hesitated. "I hate my father. He's so controlling. He wants to suppress my Indian identity. I think Matt died just to defy him. I must help free this prisoner that looks like my brother because I can't free myself. I am trapped."

"Can we get back to our meeting?" Sherrie asked.

"Yeah," Evie said smoothing her hands over the blanket. "Tell me about this blanket, Ann Marie. It's so soft. Where did you get it?"

"It's rabbit. It was my grandma's. I think she made it. The Chippewa used them for blankets, and especially for wrapping their babies. You can see how it's made from long strips of rabbit skin, then woven together. I think we should adjourn for today," Ann Marie said and abruptly stood up to leave.

"Wait a minute, don't go. Was your grandma all Indian? Mine was."

"Mine was," Sherrie said.

"So was mine," Ann Marie said, "but I gotta get going now."

"No wait," Evie said. "Maybe we should make the rabbit our *totem*, makes sense having this rabbit rug and all. What do you think?"

"It's a blanket," Ann Marie corrected.

"What's the matter with you, Ann Marie?" Evie asked. "This Spirit club was your idea in the first place."

"I didn't know you were going to go off half-cocked and actually find your brother's spirit in some prisoner. That's spooky, Evie."

Evie thought for a minute. "Don't you get it? This *proves* that we can find our ancestors' Indian Spirits."

"Matt wasn't your ancestor."

"Okay, our relatives' spirits, whatever." Dejected, Evie fingered the rabbit fur beneath her legs.

"I just didn't know you would get so carried away," Ann Marie said finally.

"So, what's a totem?" Sherrie interrupted.

"Come on, Sherrie, you never heard of a totem?" Ann Marie said.

"Don't be mean, Ann Marie," Evie said. "Explain it to her."

"Oh all right, but then I really gotta go," and she sat back down cross-legged on the blanket. "Originally, groups of Indians or clans that had a blood relationship called themselves by a designated animal. Then no one with that totem could intermarry. You know about how relatives shouldn't marry each other."

"Don't you remember when we exchanged drops of blood and became blood sisters. Now we can be a clan with a rabbit totem," Sherrie said.

"Works for me," Evie said. "How about you, Ann Marie. After all, it's your grandma's rabbit blanket."

Ann Marie shrugged in agreement. The girls rose, but Evie hurried to block their way with her back against the door.

"Now what?" Ann Marie said.

"I'm sorry—I just had to tell someone. Promise you won't say anything?" Evie pleaded.

"I promise," they said in unison.

"Let's meet next week."

The girls nodded.

Evie made up her mind to keep her new love to herself from now on.

TWENTY-ONE

COMING TO HIS SENSES WITH a blast of snow that plastered his cheek, Weston wiped his face and scanned the shoreline with his flashlight, sweeping its beam low under the trees. Brand had to be here somewhere. He stood and thrashed his way upstream against the current, the canoe tied to his belt and riding high behind him. He knew what he'd do if he were Brand caught in this storm—make a snow cave under a fallen tree, crawl into it and want to die.

He heard a noise like a moan, not quite an animal moan, more human. He couldn't tell where it was coming from, not even sure which side of the river it was on. If only the wind would subside. He quieted his movements, trying to slide through the water and listen. The canoe he'd tied to his belt rolled from side to side and pulled him back as he stumbled forward. He'd come a long way from where he'd found the abandoned canoe but was still a long distance downstream from Copper Mine Dam.

Slowly, he crept along the shore, grasping for alder bushes when his footing slipped. Above the storm, he heard a scream that sounded like it might be human and figured he was headed in the right direction.

Then came a long groan, muffled by wind and snow—as

though it were directly in front of him. He shined his light into the undercover. At first he saw the iron chain and backed off. It must be an animal after all, caught in a trap and still alive. He'd known animals, even as small a rabbit, to sound like humans screaming when trapped. He'd run into his share of those critters and had some scars to prove it. He waited and listened.

Slowly, he ran his light up the chain into a pair of eyes that burned with the wild fear of a deer felled by a pack of wolves.

"What the –"

"Don't shoot," Brand whimpered.

"Don't move, I'll get you out of here." He wished he had Peterson with him. "Hang on. I have to secure my canoe so I can crawl in there and free you."

Weston tied the canoe to a sturdy birch that hung over the water's edge, reminded that a few minutes ago this was someone he'd wished dead. He inched his way toward Brand.

What a mess, Weston thought. Brand's arm was crunched in the steel jaws of the trap. Branches framed his pitiful fetal form. Weston looked for a spot to prop the flashlight so he could see what he was doing. "This ain't going to be pretty, Brand." He grabbed a handkerchief from his coat pocket and knotted it. "Here, bite on this while I try to free you."

First, he tried opening the trap's jaws with his hands but couldn't get a good enough grip. Brand groaned in agony. Weston decided to use the handle of the canoe as a wedge to separate the jaws enough so he could hold one section down with his foot and pry open the other part with his hands. He almost got it the first time, but it snapped back.

"You okay?"

Brand had passed out. Good thing, Weston thought.

On the second try, Weston opened it far enough to wedge the paddle in further, and then next time, Weston was able to remove the metal teeth from Brand's arm and slide his arm free. It was limp, and Weston knew it must be broken.

"Now to get you out of here." He wrapped the arm in cloth-ing as best he could.

It helped that Brand was unconscious, but it didn't help to lift his dead weight. He pulled Brand toward the water as gently as he could, crawling backwards and into the river. He managed to lift Brand into the bottom of the canoe placing him on his good side and grabbed an extra rain jacket to throw over him.

The storm had gained strength, or maybe it was because he was headed into it again as he paddled downstream. Wherever he looked, snow was humped by the storm's fury. Cattails looked like cotton candy. There were no more tricky rapids to run, just shallow fast water. Mesmerized by the painter, he watched it prance alongside the canoe, jumping in the air before the waves could spit the rope back to him. The dance was hypnotizing, and they became a team, Weston along with the rope paddling to its rhythm. Once, the rope flicked back and snapped Brand's hair. He moaned. At least he was semi-conscious for now.

"We're getting closer to where we'll hole up in a cabin," Weston said.

Their silence had become a survival in communion. Brand squirmed beneath the scant jacket covering him.

Brand was alive. If only Weston could call Ryder to pick them up at Steel Bridge, but there was no way without a phone and this impassable storm. Probably no reception, anyway. He still had his gun and automatically reached for the bulge of his holster.

There wasn't much time to lose with Brand so weak and probably losing blood. It could take another hour, maybe longer with this rotten storm, to find the fishing cabin. Bad luck that a rescue at the bridge was out, but thank God for that fishing cabin. Trouble was, no one knew about it except for a few diehard fishermen, and he worried if it wouldn't be stocked with food and firewood. Weston wasn't even sure who owned the place, he'd never known. It had been there since he was a kid. Diehard local fishermen used it and kept it supplied.

It didn't take long to reach Brand's canoe, and Weston quickly lashed it to the stern. The water was shallower and wider here but too low in some spots to float over with Brand on board. Weston had to climb out several times and drag the canoe over rock ledges and gravel. At least it was easier to get his footing here where the current wasn't so strong.

He worried how long the storm would last, concerned if there was any food left in the cabin from last summer. He thought he remembered seeing some canned hash. He could always shoot a rabbit once he built a fire and got some sleep. There would be fishing poles if they had to hole up for long. Firewood was plenti-ful in the woods as long as the snow didn't get too deep.

Weston felt himself slipping into a daze and shook his head to concentrate on the river. In one sense he couldn't help dread-ing seeing the cabin again. The last time he'd been there was with Matt.

It had been fall. Matt resisted giving up a weekend of motor-cycling with his buddies to go fishing with his dad, but Weston had insisted. Matt relented. Weston called it a retreat, but Matt never bought it. Now Weston wished he'd told Matt to bring a friend along, but Weston knew why he hadn't. He wanted his son to himself. The weekend hadn't turned out as successfully as Weston had hoped. Matt never relaxed enough to get into the swing of living alone with him on the river like he had as a kid, or even two summers before. One of the arguments had been over the CD player that was plugged into Matt's ears twenty-four/seven.

"How can you hear the rapids or the wind?"

Matt shrugged and circled a finger as though he hadn't heard.

Weston retreated into himself and went fishing alone.

Finally, on the last day, it was so hot that Matt had left the cabin and gone on the river with Weston. He still had his ears plugged in to music, but he'd had fun catching fish, and afterward, they'd fileted the catch together. Weston asked Matt to fry the fish over the open fireplace at the river's edge while he cooked up some cornbread. Matt said nothing ever tasted that good. The trip had ended upbeat after all. At least Weston had that.

He had been so devastated after the accident that killed Matt, Weston could hardly remember the funeral. Best to remember the good stuff.

Matt had been a good boy, not wild, despite the rumors. It was two years now since the mid-morning call. The Douglas County sheriff was on the phone. Out on his motorcycle, hit by a car, killed, not even bad weather.

Weston stared through snow-covered pines and found himself back plowing through heavy brush near his place looking for windfalls that he and Matt had marked to fell for next year's firewood. Snow allowed for logs to be easily dragged from the forest. He felt as much at home in the woods as in the log cabin his father had built. When the whole territory was logged during the last century, somehow these white pines along the Eau Claire survived the slaughter. If ever he felt humbled, it was here where the virgin trees and the river joined forces and brought him to his knees.

It was late spring, sunny and warm before its time. They'd just waded across the Eau Claire when Matt spotted a snow-covered mound that came alive. He'd had to jump at the last minute to avoid crushing it with his boot. Curled into a ball, the tiny animal matched a clump of dried scrub oak leaves nearby.

"Abandoned, I guess."

"No wonder," Weston said. "Look at the eyes—blind."

The new-born fawn raised its head, moving its neck in a strange way.

"Listening, smelling, it's already learned that. They twist their neck like that when they can't see," Weston said. "We'd better take it home. Can you manage?"

Lifting the tiny animal in his arms, Matt nestled the furry bones against his chest. She squirmed, and he nuzzled her neck.

"Have to raise her in the barn," Weston said. "Never survive in the wild."

"Never?"

"Never."

"Let Evie name her," Matt said.

That pleased Weston. Evie could name the fawn. The distraction would be good for the kids, maybe take their minds off their mother who had recently died of cancer.

Evie named her Precious. Feeding Precious bottle after bottle until the fawn finally could eat grain and grass, Evie and Matt kept the fawn alive. It was comforting to see Evie and Matt growing closer.

Now that Matt was gone and Evie busy with high school, Weston was in charge of Precious by default. It turned out to be his daily link to Matt, and although Evie kept saying she'd do it, Weston wasn't about to relinquish the job.

Matt had wanted to build a paddock for Precious alongside the barn in hopes some buck would hop in during rutting season. Weston thought about doing it but couldn't bring himself to, so afraid another animal might harm her. Besides, it was probably too late. She might not live through a birthing and was probably too old to know how to mother a fawn after being contained in the barn since birth. He'd ended up with another prisoner.

"For your retirement," Matt and Evie had teased.

TWENTY-TWO

AFTER STEEL BRIDGE THE RIVER slowed and was deeper but no less treacherous. Boulders both seen and hidden were scattered throughout this stretch of the river. The water seemed friendlier but in reality was invisible like a wolf hidden within the brush waiting to take a fawn grazing in an opening. Huge boulders lay in waiting beneath the water. If by some mistaken read he would glide over one the wrong way, the canoe could hang up, spin 360 degrees and instantly flip. Visibility was nil. Weston used his flashlight to try and spot rocks lurking ahead. Sometimes a boulder could be detected under the surface by a swirl of water in front of it even though he couldn't see it. Usually the water was smooth as quicksilver in this stretch but not tonight. Wind whipped the black water into white-capped peaks. The canoe bobbed up and down cutting through the crests. Some had to be well over a foot high. The waves must be bouncing them right over some of those killer rocks.

It was hard paddling with the second canoe dragging behind. Sometimes it would catch up and then drop back with a jerk. Brand yelled in pain as they hit one particularly large crest, and the bow smacked down into the trough. It would be smoother once he rounded the next bend and was out of the wind. He couldn't remember a storm this vicious, especially on the St.

Croix. If they tipped over now, they would freeze to death before finding shelter.

If he zipped right past the shack without spotting it, they'd be in for it. It was small and set back from the river. He knew he had to pass a small campsite on the north side of the river, and then he would start looking along the south bank. There was no dock at the campsite or at the cabin. No pier along the St. Croix could withstand the rough winters. He thought he remembered a couple of boulders that created a place to pull in, but all that might have changed by now. Wild rivers had minds of their own.

He marveled at how Indians and trappers once depended upon this waterway daily, knew it so well whether traveling downstream to the Mississippi River or upstream to the Brule portage and on to Lake Superior. How they managed with such delicate birch bark canoes boggled his mind. He knew they patched tears with tree gum, but it must have been a constant problem. Weston had trouble enough with his modern so-called damage-proof fiberglass design. Those natives must have fought many an Alberta Clipper since it had always been a weather phenomenon even back in the fifteen/sixteen hundreds and probably before that. One thing, though, those old canoes had keels that made steering a lot easier than today's models with molded bottoms and no keel. He'd canoed as a boy with some of the native Indians on the rivers. Those rivers were tough if you shot all the rapids and didn't portage, but Indians had the knack. They never lifted their paddles from the water. Weston had practiced but never learned how to do that smooth motion in extreme conditions. He still went from side to side with his paddle when the going got rough.

Brand had been quiet for some time. The canoe wasn't bouncing around so much. The water was quieter. But the calm water was short-lived. As Weston rounded the next curve, the wind once again blew at gale force. He spotted the park camp-site on the north shore. It wouldn't be far now to the fishing cabin but knew he must go slowly so as not to miss the shack. Weston debated about pulling in at the campsite to look for firewood that was usually stacked alongside the fireplace. Campsites were always well supplied by the DNR, but he was afraid to risk taking the time. At the last minute, he changed his mind. He could pick up enough wood to heat the cabin initially. He had to go easy on his flashlight batteries so he went by instinct along the shore and spotted a narrow groove in the shore worn from canoes pulling in and out. Brand lay still as a corpse. Weston wasn't sure whether he wanted him dead or alive but was sure as hell going to save himself.

Weston hopped from the canoe, pulled it onshore a short way and lashed the painter to a tree. He wasn't up to retrieving Brand, dead or alive, floating downstream in a loose canoe. He felt his way to where he remembered the fireplace, and as he'd hoped, there was a healthy supply of split wood stashed nearby. It didn't take long to load the wood into the extra canoe. Now he wasn't so worried. At least they would be warm.

He'd stopped a few times at this campground in recent years to wait out a rain storm under an open air shelter, but there was no waiting it out tonight. This beauty was building. The snow came up to his knees as he trudged back and forth pushing his way along dragging the wood.

He knew he was close to the shack now as he shoved off down river. The temperature had to be below freezing, but it was the wind chill that frightened him. Brand was still silent, and Weston leaned forward to nudge him.

"Ugh," Brand muttered.

Still alive, Weston thought, and paddled on. Not that the storm had abated, but Weston felt better about their chances. He was almost there. At the very least they could get off the river despite what faced them in the cabin.

Forced to turn on his flashlight to see along the south shore, he maneuvered the canoe close to the shoreline. Suddenly, there was a flicker against a rock he recognized. Flashing his light up the rise, he saw the shack and heaved a sigh. It loomed before him like a temple. He headed the bow into the shore before it could float past. Once downstream, he'd have one hell of a job paddling upstream and finding where to pull in. He'd remembered two boulders but only saw one tonight.

The water was deep right up to the shore so he had to be careful not to tip the canoe as he pushed the bow onshore. Stepping into knee-deep water, he felt nothing else mattered now that he'd arrived.

Securing the canoes, he leaned over to Brand. "We made it. I'm going to open things up. Don't move. I'll be right back."

Brand lay so still Weston wondered if he was still alive, not sure he cared.

At the river's edge, snow reached well above his knees and was still coming down. Pushing his way along what he remembered as the path, he forced his body through the snow. It was a heavy snow, full of moisture, not light as when below zero in mid-winter. He reached the screen porch that faced the river and was relieved to find the door opened inward, not outward toward a huge heap of snow. Funny the things he never thought about until his survival was at stake.

The shack was open as Weston had guessed. It had never been locked in all the years he'd known but was always available to a stray fisherman who needed shelter. There had never been electricity. He managed to find a candle and matches on the shelf above a wooden table. The place looked neat enough, and there was some split wood to start the fire, but he was glad for the supply he'd brought from the campsite. Spotting a broom leaning against a weathered board wall, he propped open the door and headed back for Brand, sweeping snow aside as best he could.

Brand was awake but not coherent. The incline to the shack had not seemed steep until Weston wondered how to carry Brand.

Weston threw Brand's good arm over his shoulder, more or less standing him up, and dragged him inch by inch up the slope and into the cabin. Brand was too out of it even to moan as Weston laid him on the cot.

Relieved to be sheltered at last, Weston hadn't remembered how cold and dark the cabin could be. He was exhausted.

TWENTY-THREE

B Y THE TIME WESTON BROUGHT in the wood from the canoe and added it to the supply by the pot-bellied wood stove and lit candles, Brand had fallen asleep. Asleep or unconscious, Weston wasn't sure.

He'd never known a fire to feel this good. Hungry for the first time in many hours, he checked out food on the shelf. Not bad—oatmeal, jerky, powdered milk, coffee, canned peaches, spaghetti and lots of hash. What a find. They could last here for quite some time. The wood stove had a flat top for heating food and water. There was a Coleman stove, but Weston didn't bother to check for propane in the tank. He'd worry about that tomorrow. Although the storm still raged, the sky seemed lighter but maybe just whitened by the snow.

Taking stock of himself, he realized what a sorry trooper he was—lost both his watch and his cell phone, but they were still alive, and he planned to keep it that way.

He touched Brand's forehead and felt a raging fever. First, he had to deal with the wound.

Weston found his first-aid kit and searched for an antiseptic to clean the wound. He cut away Brand's sleeve that had twisted into a knot above the elbow and gasped at what faced him. Not only was it a nasty wound, but the bone was protruding. Lucky he hadn't bled to death. The bleeding was almost stopped. The iron teeth and his twisted sleeve had served as a tourniquet. Not sure where to start, he decided to clean the wound first before dealing with the broken bone. Brand was panting, but not fully awake.

Once Weston started washing the open wound, Brand came to life. "Gotta do this, Brand, or you won't make it." Brand fell back with a writhing grimace. Weston proceeded slowly. Once he was satisfied the wound was sterile, he went back to his supplies to bandage the area and use whatever was at hand to set the bone. It wasn't too far out of place, so Weston thought he could set the break if he could find a long enough splint to hold the bone in place. He looked around the room and spotted a broken canoe paddle. The cracked slender blade would do the trick. Now he had to prepare Brand for the pain of moving the bone back into place. He found a rag, knotted it and told Brand to open his mouth and bite down hard. Brand could hardly open his cracked lips but did as he was told.

Weston had set bones before, so he wasn't afraid to tackle this, but he was afraid of what Brand would do if he fully regained his senses. He was a mean one. Weston explained what he had to do. Brand didn't respond. When Weston forced the two bones together, Brand spit out the rag, screamed and tried to bite Weston's arm. But Weston strong-armed him, pressing him down into the cot with his knee as Brand lost consciousness. Weston managed to put the splint in place and wrap it. He'd have to wait until morning to give Brand an antibiotic. He wouldn't keep anything down tonight.

The shack was getting warm, and Brand was awake again. Weston changed into dry clothes and took Brand's wet clothes off him before wrapping him in blankets. Brand groaned as Weston begrudgingly cared for him. His years of discipline guided him to nurse Brand, but he couldn't wipe out his hatred for the inmate. Weston decided to give Brand a sedative after all, scooping water from a pail of melted snow he'd set on the stove. Brand swallowed the pill eagerly on Weston's command.

Weston breathed easier. Brand would be out for a few hours.

After he'd warmed and eaten some spaghetti, he was exhausted. Brand wasn't going anywhere, but the storm was still going strong. Weston added more wood to the stove and flopped down on his cot.

Once again his anger toward Brand surfaced. Maybe he was just too exhausted to control it. Instinctively, he hated Brand but knew that spelled trouble. For thirty years he'd trained himself to remain impartial and not let his emotions take over. It was number one in the training manual. His grandpa's warning swarmed through his head: Beware! Hate a man, and he controls you.

An eerie howl woke Weston. It sounded human. Once awake he recognized the fierce wind rubbing trees together. The sound mesmerized him, music in the wild with a beat as alive as a dozen bass fiddles tuning up. Weston settled back on the cot, lured by the strumming of the trees.

He wasn't sure how long he'd slept when a blast of frigid air woke him. Dark grey light covered the small windows facing the porch. Loud scratching and thumping made him jump to his feet to check on Brand, but he was still asleep. Then he spotted the two dark forms wrestling on the wooden table. Weston reached for his gun and moved toward the critters.

"Ya-ya!" he yelled, waving his arms to scare the animals that turned out to be a couple of pesky raccoons. He'd left the porch screen door propped open last night. The raccoons had walked in and easily pushed open the warped cabin door, eager to check out the warmth. They leapt from the table and out the door. Weston laughed at being frightened by a couple of pesky raccoons. Maybe he was getting old after all.

He stoked the stove, relieved Brand had slept through the commotion. Concerned that the wood supply wouldn't last the day, he figured he'd have to get more logs before using all the split wood. He leaned over Brand and took a closer look. He was still breathing. His temperature must have dropped, judging from the deep sleep and beads of sweat on his forehead, but Weston couldn't bring himself to touch Brand's skin. Weston flopped back onto his cot after making sure the cabin door was shut tight.

For a while he wasn't sure if he was dreaming or perhaps the nightmare was real as he writhed on his cot in a sweat. He was panting when he woke and reached for his gun, relieved to find it still bound to his armpit. Wide awake, he struggled to recon-struct the scene, to reassure himself he'd been dreaming. In his dream, he'd risen in the dark night, aimed his gun at Brand and shot him. He was afraid to look at Brand. It wasn't yet light, but Weston couldn't resist rolling over to look and find Brand on his cot, his covers ever so slightly moving up and down. He could have justified the whole thing if it had actually happened. He could say Brand had tried to kill him while he slept, broken arm and all.

TWENTY-FOUR

WHEN WESTON NEXT WOKE, the windows facing the porch seemed brighter. He roused and looked out to see the same determined storm, relentless in its pursuit. The black forest continued to sound its angelus as limbs cracked then fell silently in the snow like black phantoms in white disguise. Another time, Weston might have worshiped them.

In the faint light, Weston saw Brand lay silent, eyes wide open. He looked dead, but then he blinked.

"You had quite an adventure last night. Lucky I found you."

Brand turned his head toward the wall, muttering something inaudible sounding like, "Fuck you."

Weston ignored it. The mere sight of Brand riled him. He couldn't get past that Brand was alive, here with him, and Matt wasn't. Same age, both had Indian heritage, one alive, one dead. Weston had always believed in justice, if not in court, at the least in a controlled validation that perpetuated sanity from one day to the next, believing in all that had made sense to him—until Matt's accident. Evie said it wasn't an accident. He could-n't believe that. Matt would never have done that, taken such a risk to end his life, to no purpose.

Order was essential, yes, order, and beyond that—control of that order.

Still tired, Weston sighed heavily as Brand groaned. The fire needed more wood. Brand needed attention. Weston threw back his bed cover. Brand moaned again.

"Hang on," Weston said. Brand needed more pain medication and an antibiotic. Strange how Weston couldn't muster the energy to tend his ward. He knew he should. He looked at snow plummeting the window. What if Brand died? Would it really matter? One less loser.

Dragging himself to the stove, he clanked open the metal door and threw in a couple of logs, reminded the firewood wouldn't last long. He stood in the middle of the small cabin not sure what to do next. His stops here at the cabin had always been light-hearted following an exhausting but exhilarating day of fishing, not like this chaotic horror—after capturing an escapee. It disgusted him to think this loser had forced him out in this holocaust of a storm, probably expecting to be saved. Who would save him, Weston, if anything went wrong? No human he knew of—he counted on no one.

The logs flared as Weston stared into the red hot fire. Why was fire so mesmerizing? Stories blazed within those flames. He glanced at Brand who also stared into the fire. Weston couldn't bring himself to deny his sense of duty, despite his hatred.

"Warm enough?" he asked.

Brand didn't answer.

Suits me fine if you won't talk, Weston thought. He was going to get him out of here as soon as he could and bring him back alive and then send him back to the wall.

He turned to the shelf of food, examining what it had to offer—chicken broth, and finding a can opener put the opened can of soup on the stove top. "Won't be long," he muttered more to himself than Brand.

Brand groaned in anticipation as Weston brought soup to feed him. He could hardly contain himself. "Not too fast,"

Weston warned. "You gotta keep this down so I can give you some medicine."

Seated on a straight wooden chair next to Brand's cot, Weston looked down at the apparatus he'd constructed to set the broken arm. Impressed with his hastily improvised cast, he checked to make sure nothing was too tight. "Still hungry?" Weston asked, and Brand nodded. "That's a good sign."

Weston plodded back to the supply shelf. "Well, what sounds good? Oatmeal, hash, sweet potatoes, oatmeal, hash, sweet potatoes, oatmeal?"

"Sweet potatoes," Brand said in a raspy whisper. "And water."

Weston stalled for time to make sure Brand would keep the soup down. He primed the pump at the sink with melted snow and brought over a glass of water along with an antibiotic pill. Brand heaved forward to swallow. The kid is tough, Weston thought, and went back to find the pain medication. Once Brand had swallowed that, Weston decided he should wait to introduce the sweet potatoes.

Weston had never been into feeding his kids as infants. But he remembered watching his wife introduce new foods one at a time. The only feeding Weston had known of late was making sure Precious was well fed. He hoped Evie hadn't forgotten to feed her.

"Gotta piss," Brand said.

"I put a container by your bed. You can reach it with your good arm." Weston wasn't about to lower himself to hold a piss pot for a bum.

Weston checked out the wood supply. It might last the next few hours, but he was too tired to go out and find wood right now. Brand would have to wait for the sweet potatoes. As soon as he'd fixed the fire, Weston flopped down on his cot to sleep, hoping Brand would fall back asleep.

Sometimes when he was this tired, he couldn't get to sleep. But tonight he felt himself drift into oblivion.

TWENTY-FIVE

Brand tossed and turned as he'd watched Weston's blanketed form highlighted by a glow from the stove rise and fall with each breath. Despite the pain in his arm, Brand drifted in and out of a nightmarish dream but couldn't break out of his god-damned dream state. Maybe he'd gone crazy. Prior to prison, he'd taken plenty of drugs, uppers, downers, but nothing had spun him into this topsy turvy catapult he felt under Weston's control. The medicine didn't really knock him out, only temporarily dulled the pain. Problem was, he was climbing the wall.

He watched through slits in his eyes as Weston poked at the fire in the pot-bellied stove adding another log, maneuvering it to flame just the right amount. The pain medication kicked in full force, and he could breathe again.

Weston hated him, and Brand knew it, despite the care Weston was giving him. Even though Weston had set Brand's broken arm, fed him, helped him pee, eased his pain, Brand could taste Weston's hatred. It blanketed Brand like a sixth sense. He'd lived with hate. It was his mantra, first from his Mama. Funny how he could remember the fear of being hated by her but couldn't remember how she looked. She had to have been a half-breed because he did remember she wasn't dark enough to be full-blooded Indian. His dad, though he'd never seen him, must have been half-Indian, too, judging from his own light color. He was never sure who the woman he called "Auntie" was before he was sent to a foster home where they beat him and wouldn't feed him. It wasn't long before he ran away to live on the street. Out on the bricks was where he'd honed his skills. It was where he'd learned to sniff out hatred. It was the stench of garbage and deep fried grease all mixed in with hate. He kept adding to the list. Weston was the latest addition—and Dollar Bill. He couldn't forget that ass-hole.

Watching and waiting, he had become an animal, ready to act on cue. He must think like an animal if he was going to survive. So he cast his eyes about as if he were in the wild.

Maybe Weston was planning to let him die after all. Weston could get away with anything out here, even murder.

He resolved to outsmart him. When he lay in the snow-covered cave, his arm encased in steel jaws, he felt what it was to be trapped like an animal. Now he was going to figure out how to free himself, how to escape. He shivered under the blanket.

Weston put on his coat to go outside.

"Gotta pee?"

Brand shook his head. "I'm cold."

Weston felt his forehead. "You have a fever again. Let me bring in some wood, and I'll give you some aspirin."

Brand snuggled beneath his blankets away from the blast of frigid air as Weston opened the door. Who was this man? Brand wondered. Did he have kids, a wife—was he human, for God's sake? Why had he bugged him relentlessly at the prison? He hadn't badgered the other prisoners. Besides, Brand hadn't done anything to provoke him.

The kinder Weston treated him here at the cabin, the more Brand distrusted him. What was he going to do next—feed him—fatten him up for the kill? Maybe at some point he'd let him accidentally drown. But why wouldn't he have done that before—right after he'd found him on the river? It would have been easy. Maybe Weston would taunt him to death like a cat does with a mouse, forcing him to self destruct. He'd seen a TV show like that where a cop dangled a man from an upper story window with a rope over and over until the man jumped to his death of his own free will.

He squeezed his eyes tight shut and tried to escape in sleep. He wished he'd memorized every minute of the beginning of the river trip. He struggled to relive it, what it felt like, the warm breeze, the sounds. He'd never known anything like it. He actually he could see the ripples on the water against his eyelids, the eagle and the yellow leaves, everything so very, very yellow. Death coursed through him again. It was an ache in his bones. He'd never been happy. What was happy anyway? He clung to the image of the girl. But was it the girl or had a phantom ghost come to haunt him?

Suddenly he was being squeezed into a place he didn't want to go, crawling through a cave, and he was stuck, unable to breathe, his nose pressed against rock. He panicked in waves. His mind leapt from being lured to screaming. When he woke, he was sweating and knew he hadn't been fully asleep. He couldn't shake the horrible image of passing from an expanse to being squeezed into a confined passage, too small to breathe.

Branches cracked in the forest like gun shots as they snapped from their trunks. He strained but couldn't hear them land, no finality to their death. How deep was the snow now? Through the window overhead he saw the storm still raging. Snowflakes swirled against the pane, and now and then a blast of wind shook the glass and sent cold air down his neck. It didn't help his despair. He wanted to die right now. When Weston returned, he'd find him dead and wouldn't have the pleasure of watching him slowly die. If he made it out of here, he'd never trust another cop, not that he ever had, except for Ryder. He kind of liked Ryder. Too bad Ryder wasn't with Weston now. What had made Weston come out in this storm alone—to kill him, that's what. Otherwise, he would have brought someone along to help him. Now he was sure of it. If only he had a gun.

He must have dozed off because he felt calmer when he roused, but it was horrible to wake up to this white caged world. This was the last place he wanted to be, and he felt like crying. He was ashamed and hungry, had to pee, and in horrible pain again. Please let him die. Then he remembered the girl, his girl. Now that he had touched her, she was his. He would force himself to live. He would get his strength back and find her. He cursed himself for not carrying her back into the house and making love. How bright the day had been. Her hair had shone where the sun touched it. He'd had her in his very hands. The imagined sight of her soft mouth curving to her cheekbones, her tight white tank top with the tiny straps, her short, short blue jeans, and her sexy red toenails—bright, bright red—made him desperate. He tried to picture how her breasts felt, but he couldn't be sure if he actually touched them. He cried, longing to capture her nipples. How could he not remember any of this. Shit! How could he forget the most important thing in his life! His brain must be fried.

He wiped his eyes on the edge of the blanket with his good hand before Weston could wake and see him. He felt around the floor for the bottle to pee but couldn't reach it.

TWENTY-SIX

WAKING WITH A START, Weston suddenly remembered where he was and quickly looked to see what Brand was doing. He seemed to be sound asleep.

Weston shoved his way out the door and pushed snow from the porch using the flimsy broom to clear away the snow. The path he'd made a few hours before was all but covered, but he persevered sweeping his way down the cabin steps and around the corner, forcing his way along side the cabin toward the back where he prayed he would still find some logs in the woodpile. He'd never known it to be totally depleted, but it was the end of the season, and there had been some cold weather recently when someone might have used up the supply and not restocked it.

The cabin was bounded by spruce planted years ago that complained as sudden gusts of wind contorted everything in sight. It was snowing harder. Weston shivered, hoping the colder temperature meant the storm was abating. Maybe he was just tired and feeling it more. He'd never been out in an Alberta Clipper for so long and wished he'd memorized more of the survival stories he'd heard. He'd always thought they were exaggerated until now. It would have been a plus to have Peterson with him, but he couldn't worry about that now.

If only he'd paid more attention to what his father had said about the Alberta Clippers he'd survived or perhaps listened to his wife's Indian tales. Maybe he should make that a project in his retirement—collect Alberta Clipper stories. He liked the idea of living in the past. Everything had already happened, pre-dictable, not so scary. Maybe that's why there were so many con-firmed historians. History was safe.

Snow crept to his crotch as he thrust his body forward inching along, swinging his legs from the hip. The storm was gaining force, no question. Soft-packed snowballs splatted against his face.

The wood pile wasn't as hard to uncover as he'd feared. He couldn't believe his good fortune when he found nearly a full cord of pine and oak neatly stacked. He hadn't remembered this. Normally chipmunks would scamper from the woodpile when he approached. They must be deep in hiding, and he won-dered how hungry he'd have to get to eat a chipmunk just as one surfaced and dove headlong into the snow. He wasn't worried about the chipmunks, they'd make it fine through the storm, find an air pocket and live to see spring.

With each armload of logs he carried back to the cabin porch, Weston looked longingly at the river. After what he decided was his last load, he couldn't resist making his way to the river's edge. It had snowed so much since they arrived, he could barely see where he'd dragged Brand to the cabin. One measured time by storms like this dating weddings, deaths and births before or after an Alberta Clipper.

At the water's edge, he realized nothing changed where the river was concerned. Storms came and went, but rocks beneath the surface still controlled the water's path. Whether fish or flotsam, the current was the boss. The river surged past him, had for centuries. He tried to imagine himself the first person to have seen this waterway. Although Indians were the first, each subsequent first-time visitor must have been awed. It produced reverence. He knew the Chippewas used this waterway like he used the roads and then wondered how they handled an Alberta Clipper. Did they simply hole up or did they use it as a cover to ambush some Sioux settlement?

In a strange way, he liked the smallness of this white world, escaping the confusion of the larger picture. He should bring the preacher here some time and let him sense this power first hand. It was stronger than all the words he preached from the Bible.

If the storm weren't blocking his view, he would be able to see across the river where he'd put a foothold on a rock and cast the shore many times. Last time was with Matt. They'd caught their limit of bass and a couple of walleye that late afternoon. He'd never forget. So what if they hadn't spoken. What he managed to remember was never recorded in words anyway.

There weren't too many things he could count on not to change, but thank God the river was a constant. He could accept the effect of attrition—that took centuries. However, now that he thought about it, he wasn't so sure. Sure, the river was always there, but the water was always new—never the same water. The water was constantly being renewed. He liked that idea even though the mere thought of change angered him.

His tight control at the prison had worked until recently, but now they demanded changes in the routine. Change meant laxity, laziness in his book. It took no effort to look the other way. Why not let the inmates dictate prison life—change the dress code—whatever—give an inch. He couldn't abide it.

Precious was another given in his world. But it scared him to think he might lose Evie. Her words still reverberated, "Matt was playing that chicken game—race across the highway without looking and take the chance that no car was coming." Weston couldn't accept that. He'd taught Matt that living demanded control, leaving little to chance.

Here by the river, time had become unstitched, but he knew it was the storm that did it—a paradox with its pounding wind and snow along with the muffled silence it produced. The storm had swallowed them whole, held them in exile. No cry could permeate the whiteness. Echoes fell dead.

The river mesmerized him. Even though the ribboned water reflected his face as disfigured, he gave in to it because he trusted that its rules never changed. He stared down as the dark liquid lapped up each snowflake as though dying of thirst. Snow collected along the bank but quickly dissolved with the lightening flick of a rippled wave. Cattails flailed in the wind. Steam rose from the river as though nature was hallucinating. Barely visible through the clotted mist a huddle of frightened ducks floated past like small ghosts who should have departed long ago.

The native Indians managed to survive these storms. Old Chief Kabamappa had lived a long life in a teepee. Bad as this was, at least Weston had a cabin for protection.

If Brand got sicker, and they had to hole up much longer, he'd have to catch fish and pull cattail bulbs to cook. He'd eaten them as a boy. He thought he remembered they had some medicinal effect. This melee would produce no fish, however. The weather would have to change for the fish to bite.

Change, a word he hated, but it loomed on the horizon in the form of retirement. He could handle that. He'd do all the things he loved like hunting and fishing day in and day out, no surprises.

Lost in the moment, he'd forgotten the problem at hand, then stiffened, dreading what was caged in the cabin. He was ashamed to admit he felt threatened by the sick, wounded prisoner. This escape had definitely put a damper on his stellar record at the prison.

He figured he would keep Brand sedated until he recovered enough to canoe him to the state line where law enforcement would be waiting. It seemed simple enough. He had plenty of medication, food and wood to keep them alive for several days.

A lone water bug zigzagged across the water's surface retracing its effort to escape the snow and ice. Weston had no idea how long he'd been standing by the river.

TWENTY-SEVEN

WESTON STOMPED HIS BOOTS in front of the cabin door and brushed snow from his clothes before carrying in the load of wood. Dumping it by the stove, he glanced at Brand who pointed to the urine bottle on the floor.

"So?" Weston said.

"Can't reach it."

Weston used his boot to shove it within reach. Bad enough to empty it. When he'd finished, Weston took the bottle from Brand on his way to the porch for more wood. The urine was darker than it should be, but he'd keep an eye on it and make sure he drank more water. After stoking the fire, Weston walked over to check on his patient. Brand felt hot so he gave him more aspirin.

"Hungry?"

Brand nodded.

Brand seemed especially docile, but Weston knew better than to trust him. God only knew what he'd pull next. In any event, he'd keep him sedated until he could load him in the canoe and paddle down to the next bridge. As soon as the storm subsided, Ryder would have a patrol there, if not himself.

Weston opened a can of vegetable soup along with some hash and set the cans on top of the stove to heat. He'd give

Brand another pain pill as soon as he'd eaten and follow it up with a sleeping pill. He couldn't take any chances with this wild animal.

After they'd eaten, Weston decided to take another look at the wound. He grabbed a rag from the pile of sheets he'd ripped into strips. Much as he considered Brand scum, it surprised him to find himself caring for Brand as if he were his own son. Unable to divorce himself from the survival routine, he stuck to the rules he'd learned over the past thirty-five years.

It was getting hot in here. The storm hadn't ended and produced a cold wave yet. He lifted the blankets from Brand and reached for his arm. Brand jerked before Weston could touch him.

"I need to check the wound again, make sure it's healing."

Brand relaxed, and Weston moved closer to unwind the makeshift bandage that held the canoe paddle in place. As he exposed the wound, Brand swore at him.

"I should be an expert by now," Weston said. "Have you ever broken a bone before?"

Brand shook his head.

"Well, I've set my share of broken bones."

It was hard being so close to someone he hated and yet looked so much like his son. He wondered if Matt had sensed someone caring for him when he was badly hurt after the accident. Had he been too out of it, or was there no one there to help him? Weston hadn't been called until it was too late, too late to comfort his dying son.

As long as Weston could remember, he'd been intrigued with law enforcement. His folks hadn't been so keen on it, but Weston persevered. At one point, Weston's dad had been a guard at the prison. Then he'd left the prison to work for Safeway Foods at their warehouse in Superior. Weston never knew why, probably better pay. Maybe he thought it was safer. But then one day a truck at the Safeway loading ramp lost its brakes and backed right over Weston's father. His father died before Weston's high school graduation, leaving Weston to support his mother. So much for safer. Weston knew he could make a good living at law enforcement and could rise within the ranks. His dad had wanted him to go to automotive school.

"Cars are here to stay," he'd said.

Weston knew his dad was right, but "so is crime," he'd countered. Something in him wanted to put the human side of the world in order. Maybe it was his awe of nature's control over mankind and why humans didn't cooperate. He hadn't been able to tell his dad exactly what all that had meant to him, and he wasn't sure he could even explain today after all these years in law enforcement. It simply felt right.

"Am I hurting you?"

Brand grimaced.

Weston sterilized the area with spray from the medicine kit. "Looks good," he said and bandaged it again. "You keep doing this well, we can head out soon as the storm's over."

Brand looked away sheepishly. Weston couldn't figure the attitude, must be the medication, and decided to up the dose.

"Am I going to die?" Brand asked.

Weston wasn't about to offer too much hope. "I don't know."

Brand turned to the wall and muttered, "Shit."

Weston checked out the food supply again, satisfied the cans of soup, beans, and stew would last a few more days. Brand's eyes looked heavy, so Weston decided he could safely take a short nap. He couldn't remember being this exhausted. Making sure his gun was lodged beneath his clothing, he flopped onto the cot, keeping the gun concealed beneath his body.

Brand tried to sleep but was crawling the wall again. It had to be the medication. He needed to plan an escape. Just like Weston to overdose him. First of all, he decided he was not going to resist. He would comply and act tame as a kitten. Weston was going to kill him the first chance he had, Brand knew it. He had to outsmart him, but he couldn't do that if he continued to take the drugs Weston was forcing on him. Brand listened as Weston fell into a deep sleep snore. He would memorize the pattern.

TWENTY-EIGHT

"DO YOU GET LONESOME?" Brand called out to Weston. Weston thought he was dreaming. "What's that?"

"Do you get lonesome?"

Weston jerked to a sitting position. He thought he'd put Brand out for a long spell.

Weston was too busy to be lonesome, but he did worry about feeling alone. He'd always had the Buckhorn. Most of the time he felt welcome there. It was a third place where he belonged, not just to drink, but to meet friends, shoot the breeze. He had home, work and this third place and Evie. He stretched his body long and rolled up to a sitting position.

Brand turned toward the wall. "I just wondered."

Weston rose and shivered. It was none of Brand's business whether or not he felt lonesome. What was Brand up to anyway — asking personal questions of a prison superintendent?

He walked to the stove, opened the fire door and shoved a couple of logs in place, poking at them to break into a flame. He had no right to be angry, but he continued to seethe in Brand's presence. Maybe because Brand threatened his future, but he wasn't going to let that happen. Weston paced the cabin's limited square footage. "Can't sit still," he said to the walls. "Never could."

Weston grabbed his coat to get some more wood. It was only mid-afternoon but already almost dark. The snow showed no signs of letting up. Stubborn storm, Weston grumbled.

He forged his way through the snow that had once again all but blocked the meager path he'd been tracing back and forth to the woodpile behind the cabin. He knocked snow from the top of the pile and loaded his arms with as much wood as he could handle. The way back should be a little easier.

As he turned, he heard Brand's scream. Weston dropped his load, stumbling through the snow to the porch entrance. The porch and cabin doors were wide open. Entering the small square room, Weston saw the critter. A bear cub was making its way through the supplies and about to climb on to the long bench that doubled as a table beneath the supply shelves. Weston relaxed as he moved toward Brand on his cot.

"Don't worry, it's just a cub, looks like a year-end cub left alone, disoriented by the storm."

Weston waved his arms yelling, "Hyah! Hyah! Out a here!"

"Help," Brand screamed.

"That's right, keep screaming. That'll scare him."

Suddenly, a huge black form filled the doorway. Brand screamed louder and rolled into a ball on the cot, hiding his head. It was the mother sow in search of her cub. She clacked her teeth. Weston knew what that meant. She was not only surprised but frightened. Weston moved to Brand's side of the cabin to make room for the bears' escape.

"Stand up," Weston commanded Brand as he huddled together on the cot. "Wave your arms, both of them. She'll be frightened by something big and loud. Scream, dammit!"

Brand lay immobile in a coil on his cot.

The stove separated them from the bears, and Weston knew no bear would mess with a fire. It had died down, but the pot belly was still warm. Brand whimpered as Weston reached for the urine bottle and poured its contents in a line along the floor in front of them.

Brand recoiled.

"It's a threat, like a fire wall," Weston said.

Weston had a gun hidden beneath his clothes but hesitated to reveal it. Brand was just as wild as these bears if not more so. He would use the gun as a last resort. Besides, Brand would know the minimum security prison used no guns to confine or threaten prisoners, and he wouldn't know for sure if Weston had a gun.

The sow busied herself smelling along the side of the cabin where the food was kept. Now that she had found her cub, she stopped every so often to make a loud threatening blowing sound. It was as though Weston and Brand weren't even there, but he knew the sound effects were meant for them. She nosed the canned goods, rolling them over onto the table and floor, then sniffed her way to the open cracker tin. One paw tipped it on edge, and they quickly devoured the crackers. Making their way along the shelves, the pair knocked over dishes, pots and pans right and left. With one deft swat the sow sent a large can of stew smashing against the wall across the room, but not hard enough to spew the contents. Weston felt Brand's shaking the cot with every crash to the floor. At least something had his respect, Weston thought.

Most of their food was sealed in cans. A variety of grunts accompanied the forage as though they were having a conversation. It took ten to fifteen minutes for the bears to scour back and forth the shelves and the table.

"I thought they were afraid of people," Brand whispered finally able to sit up.

"They're probably confused by the early storm." Weston grabbed Brand under the arm and pulled him to his feet on the cot. "Act brave."

Here we are, Weston thought, two enemies teamed up against two bears. It was laughable.

Actually, Weston wasn't all that worried about their safety. He knew the bears would soon get bored with their search for food and amble outside to continue their foraging for food and a place to hole up for winter.

Weston admired the handsome sow. Her head was unusually large with huge ears. She was probably young enough that her body was still catching up to her head. Something in the bear's spirit connected with him. What was it thinking? Planning an attack on its prey? Weston and Brand had become the prey. Weston imagined thinking like the bear, disoriented from the storm, desperately needing food before the winter sleep, fearlessly protecting an offspring—doing a better job than he had for Matt. Over the years, he'd learned a lot from bears. They had few enemies and were in control of their world. Weston envied their confident freedom, no slinking around. Hunting season was their only enemy. Bears were no match for the end of a gun barrel. Weston couldn't abide bear hunting with dogs and radio collars.

He admired how skillfully the bear manipulated its paws, turning over one item after another to smell and examine it. "Look at that," he whispered to Brand who'd once again covered his head with his arms. "Look how adept she is."

One time he'd watched a bear pick a blackberry patch clean using its claws to pull a branch to its mouth, extracting one berry at time with its front teeth. He'd also seen a bear deftly skin the carcass of a deer not yet recovered by some hunter who'd given up the chase. It ate everything, hooves and all except for the skin and fur. The only live prey he'd seen bears take was very young fawns. He'd seen that several times. Or mice, a bear couldn't resist a mouse. After years of encounters Weston had learned the bear's language, sensing which grunts meant what. Most bears were big bluffers when put to the test, but this one was too close for comfort.

Finally, the sow found a partially used can of Crisco and managed to remove the plastic cover. The cub joined her. She shared the find. There was little else left to eat that wasn't sealed or canned, and Weston wondered what she'd do next. Before giving up, the bear went to the garbage pail, and the two of them licked clean every can Weston had discarded.

Suddenly, the sow turned on Weston and Brand. Weston jumped up to stand on the cot, raised his arms and howled at her. He'd been close to many a bear, but this one loomed especially large, taking up a huge space in the small cabin. Judging from the angle of her head, she acted as though she might advance—then she made a sudden lunge. She huffed and coughed moving in on them. Then lunged again. Weston raised his head and howled like a wolf in pursuit. It had little effect on her attitude except to stop her. Black bears were renowned bluffers. The cub didn't move, poised behind its mother. As the sow rose on her hind legs, her head almost brushed the rough-hewn ceiling. She feigned a step toward Weston, clacking her teeth. Brand screamed. Seeming to sense heat from the stove, the sow retreated, slowly dropping on all fours in slow motion. She turned to leave.

Weston relaxed enough to sense how the scene had shifted. He wasn't used to being preyed upon.

Suddenly, the sow stopped and faced Weston. She raised her snout, sniffed about and unleashed an explosive burst like an Alberta Clipper gust rushing through the cabin. Weston waved his arms overhead and countered with a wolf-like howl. Slowly, the grand animal shifted her gaze out the door as though being called by the storm. She emitted several non-threatening grunts as though talking to her cub.

Methodically placing one paw before the other, she padded her way toward the open cabin door, signaled another grunt to her cub and ambled onto the porch. The cub dutifully followed its mother down the steps and out into the stormy night. Snow covered their escape. By the time Weston rushed to close the porch and cabin doors, they were out of sight. It amazed him how such large creatures could vanish so quickly.

TWENTY-NINE

Brand lay in a coil on the cot as though still in shock. The fire was all but out. Two logs remained. Weston shoved them onto the few remaining coals. He'd wait a little before going out to the woodpile allowing their furry guests time to retreat into the woods. He hated to admit his heart was still racing.

Weston started cleaning up the mess the bears had made, actually pleased they'd found a little nourishment to face the winter. The storm would force them to hibernate soon. They would find good cover beneath branches the storm had stripped from trees.

"Can't we lock the door?" Brand asked.

"There is no lock, we'll brace a chair against the handle tonight."

"Why not now?"

"Relax, they're done with us." Weston retrieved a can of stew from a corner of the room, opened it and set it on the stove. "Hungry?"

"Not really."

Weston pulled his first aid kit from under his cot and unwrapped Brand's wound. Thank God he'd remembered in his rush to bring along the medicine kit, sedatives and all. Now that Brand was improving, he'd have to sleep on the meds to hide them.

"Shit!" Brand cringed from Weston's touch.

Weston frowned at the redness surrounding the injury. "This needs soaking." Actually, he was pleased at how well the bone seemed to be setting, but the infection worried him.

He put a pan of water on the stovetop next to the can of stew. He'd keep soaking and treating the wound with an antibiotic, and hopefully, the storm would stop soon enough to get Brand to a hospital. Weston surprised himself. When treating Brand's wound, his anger strangely subsided, but once he turned away to heat the water, resentment crept back into his soul.

Weston lay down on his cot and closed his eyes. It was as if Matt had reappeared in the form of this creep—this loser. The voice—even the build—hair plastered to the forehead. He couldn't stop comparing them. He felt Matt's presence almost more than when Matt was alive. It was unbearable. For months Matt had been with him, if not perched on his shoulder, constantly in his mind. He looked over at this bum that resembled Matt so much it was scary.

He hated Brand all the more for it. Let him lie there and rot. What did he care.

"You gonna leave my arm open like this?"

"'Til the water heats. Shut up and lie still."

Weston turned a deaf ear to Brand's whimpering. He couldn't bring himself to feel sorry for him. Still, it had taken a lot of guts for him to escape, and who knows, he probably would have made it if the storm hadn't hit. Weston wondered who had helped him. How did he know where to steal a canoe? He couldn't figure. He'd find out eventually but knew better than to grill him until the proper time. He couldn't afford to be accused of coercion, another example of going soft on prisoners. When he started working in the system, that wouldn't have been an issue. He'd have gotten everything out of him by now.

"You married?" Brand blurted out.

"What do you care?"

"Just wondered."

Weston considered not answering. Maybe the kid would shut up if he answered. "I was, my wife died, so quit wondering."

"Don't you miss sex?"

That did it. Weston went out to pick up the wood he'd dropped and cool off.

The weather hadn't changed one whit, snow continued to mount. It depressed him. Maybe he'd end up dying here, holed up with this despicable specimen of humanity. He was ashamed to claim the same species with him.

He looked to the sky and let snowflakes fall on his face, soothed by the cool wetness. What a relief from the stench of the overheated cabin.

There was no evidence of the bears' invasion, not even a footprint. He wasn't worried about the bears. Maybe he wouldn't survive, but he knew the bears would. He loaded his arms with the logs he'd dropped earlier when Brand had screamed, and he'd rushed back to the cabin.

Once inside, he stoked the stove, checking the status of the stew and the water pot. Both needed more heat.

"See the bears?"

"Course not. They're smarter than we are."

Weston sat down on a chair and pulled it near the stove.

"Do you miss sex?" Brand asked again.

"Think I'm going to answer that?"

"I have a girlfriend."

"I'm glad."

"No, seriously. She's a gorgeous girl."

"I wish her luck."

"How about me? Don't you wish me luck?"

Weston hunched down, his arms resting on his legs. He found no words to express what he felt. Not even to himself, let alone to

Brand. He hadn't been able to talk to Matt, mainly because Matt wouldn't talk, but this butt-ass was suddenly a talker. How to shut him up? He must be feeling a lot stronger. He'd ignore him.

"Do you have children, a son maybe or a daughter?"

"If you ask me that again, I swear I will kill you."

"Can we eat?"

"I have to dress your wound."

Weston roused himself to tear some strips from a spare sheet, dropped a strip in the hot water and carried it over to the cot. It was too hot and Brand swore at him, but Weston lost himself in soaking the wound. Once again as he nursed Brand, his hatred melted. His change in attitude baffled him. He felt peaceful. He spent more time than was needed to place and replace the poltices on the reddened area, then patted it dry and squeezed antibiotic ointment on the wound.

Weston was aware of Brand watching him finish the bandaging. "You're a pro at that."

Weston rose to dish up their stew wondering how many more meals of stew he could down. He'd have to remember to restock the cabin but with more canned fruit and vegetables.

Weston handed Brand his plate. "I think you can sit at the table."

Brand broke the silence saying, "I'm gonna do something different when I get out, something new."

Weston laughed. "First of all, it's going to be a while til you *get out*, and secondly, there's nothing new in the world except what's been forgotten. My grandpa told me that. You'd do well to remember that."

"How do you know about my son?" Weston demanded later. "I don't."

Weston's head ached. What made him think Brand had mentioned Matt? Had Matt left him in the lurch and maybe climbed on this loser's back? Would he have to take the two of them on?

"So what *do* you want to be?" Weston asked out of boredom.

152

"A man, not a half-breed."

Weston never thought of Matt as a half-breed, but here he was holed up with this half-breed, and Matt had slipped off his back. Weston jumped up from his cot and paced the room.

"Do you ever think there's a plan for us, all of us, I mean," he suddenly blurted, "out there somewhere?"

Brand laughed. "Scares the hell out of me."

"Like a pre-planned design."

"If there's some fucking design, then control it. You control everything else, don't you?"

"Don't use foul language with me. There's no one here to impress, no one can hear you. Why don't you speak English anyway—you smart guys—you all think you're so smart—no one understands what you say."

"That's the pre-planned design," Brand laughed.

"Don't laugh—don't you dare laugh at me."

"I was laughing at me, some plan, like you said."

"Right, some plan, look where it got you—stranded on a river in the worst Clipper of the century with a broken arm. Some smart plan. Tell me this, Mr. Smarts, how's the world going to get along if we can't understand each other? Explain that."

"I understand all I need to know."

"What kind of answer is that?"

"Everybody lies."

"What does that mean, other than smart talk? Besides, it's rude."

"You lie, I lie."

"You keep inventing stuff with this street talk."

"Gotta keep up."

"That's nonsense, you're talking nonsense. How are we going to get along if we don't speak the same language?" Weston shouted.

Brand was quiet and stared at the floor. "We'd find a way," he said.

"What do you mean, a way to what?"

"Some way to hate each other."

"Do you hate me?"

"Of course. Everybody hates you. I gotta' hate you."

"I saved your life."

Brand buried his head in his free arm. "You should'a let me die out there—I ain't gonna live long anyway—never get old like you."

"We need to change your language. That would be a start."

"No one would understand me," Brand laughed.

Weston poked his finger at his own chest. "I would," he yelled, red-faced. "And I'm the one that counts."

Weston rose to collect their plates. "My wife was an Indian, for God's sake," he said aloud.

"I didn't know that."

So it's not about race, Weston thought, his hatred of Brand. Still, he knew he barely tolerated certain people. Weak men, and liars, couldn't abide them.

"Tell me about her," Brand said.

"Who?" Weston asked as though in a trance.

"Your wife. Did you love her?"

Weston stared at the glow through slots in the stove door. A yellow light flickered about the bare cabin. It had been a long time since he'd heard that word said out loud. "Love?" he repeated the word to himself. The word warmed the room. He'd loved his wife but couldn't remember when he'd said it out loud. He could never bring himself to say 'I love you.' Somehow to say it, cheapened it, negated it. If someone said that to him, he's not sure he'd believe it. Love was something you showed, not talked about.

"You fuck her a lot?"

Weston had lost the spunk to reprimand Brand. "We had two kids, but my boy died." Just saying that—"my boy died"—broke something loose. Something went *tic* in his brain.

"How come?"

"Motorcycle accident—can't talk about it." Evie had said he'd tried to control Matt like she thought Weston controlled her.

Brand changed the subject. "My girlfriend loves me. She said so, and she kissed me like she meant it."

Weston refused to follow this conversation and rose to get more wood. "I think you can pee off the front porch from now on."

Back inside the cabin, Weston stacked the wood next to the stove and made himself a cup of coffee. Was there no end to this?

THIRTY

B RAND LAY ON HIS COT PROPPED up by his good arm. "I got a question for you."

"I'll bet you do," Weston snapped.

"What's with this ancient Indian settlement on the St. Croix?"

"Where'd you hear about an ancient Indian village?" Weston asked.

"I saw it –in the prison library—on a map."

So, Weston thought, Brand did have a plan all along, but he knew better than to interrogate him out here alone in the wilderness. He would wait until there were witnesses. A map— of the river—in the prison library? He'd have to remember to check on those books in the library.

"What do you want to know?" Weston asked.

"Was there an ancient Indian village?"

"Yes. There were quite a few scattered on or near the St. Croix."

"Tell me. I'm Indian. I want to know."

"I don't know a lot. Indians didn't write anything down, but they had fantastic memories. What I know about the settlement goes back more than one hundred and fifty years according to journals written by Indian agents that passed through the area between 1820 and 1850. It's actually kind of sad."

Weston stopped to think. He'd never thought of the Chippewa's history as sad. He couldn't believe he was telling this saga, but it had always interested him.

"What do you mean, sad?" Brand asked.

"Because the chief of that village, Chief Kabamappa, caused his own downfall."

Weston poured his coffee and sat near the stove facing Brand. He leaned his elbows on his legs and gazed into the coffee mug. He hadn't thought of old Kabamappa for some time, but when he was a kid, Kabamappa had been a favorite tobacco-chewing topic when the old-timers gathered at the Buckhorn. In fact, Weston hung around just to hear more about the old Indian. He'd always wondered if Maria had been a descendent of Kabamappa. He knew Indians from that village had intermarried with loggers and trappers once they moved into the area.

"Where was this Kabakaba village?" Brand asked.

"Kabamappa," Weston corrected. "In the swampy lake section of the river, a mile or so above the dam."

"Go on," Barnes urged now, sitting up on his cot.

"For centuries the Chippewas in the St. Croix Valley had lived exactly the same way—hunting deer, beaver, otter, bear, rabbits, birds, dependant on their meat, skins and feathers. Kabamappa was a Chippewa. They gathered wild rice in the fall from the St. Croix flowage and planted corn, potatoes, and pumpkins in the summer. No Big Macs."

"Sounds boring," Brand said. "How many lived in that village?"

"One agent's report said there were eighty-three in Chief Kabamappa's clan, twenty-five men, the rest were women and children. They had their problems, though. It seems the Sioux and the Chippewas were constantly invading and killing each other. Centuries ago the Chippewas were pushed westward by the feisty Iroquois in the East, and the Chippewas ran into the Sioux or Dakotas as they were called and then forced them westward. The Sioux didn't take kindly to that. So for many,

many years they continued to raid each other's villages, attack a hunting party or a lone Indian whenever they had the chance. It was hard to even the score so they just kept avenging the murder of this Sioux or that Chippewa."

"Sounds insane."

"Well, it was in a way, but they couldn't figure out how to end it. I'll bet you've had it in for somebody, and then when you retaliated, they could hardly wait to get back at you. Same thing. In fact, each clan trained their young braves not only to hunt animals but mainly to be warriors. It seems it was a lot more fun to go on a warring party than a hunting party. There was a scalping pole right there in Kabamappa's settlement."

"Scalping?"

"That was how the warriors gained esteem, coming home with Sioux scalps. That was horrible. There were plenty of peace pipe meetings, but the peace never lasted, and the first thing you knew they'd have at it again. But there was a funny twist I have never quite understood. It seems if a Sioux who had murdered a Chippewa was caught, he wasn't always killed in retribution. Sometimes they brought the murderer home, and the family of the murdered adopted him as a family member."

"Instead of scalping?"

"I guess maybe it was a kind of replacement for the lost son." Weston finished his coffee. "We better get some sleep."

"No, I want to hear about Mapakapa's downfall," Brand insisted.

"It's Kabamappa, and I'll tell you tomorrow."

Weston gave Brand his goodnight pill, tipped a chair against the door handle and flopped onto his cot.

Before succumbing to sleep, Weston reran the scenario of the she-bear in the cabin, her coat shining in the glow of the candle, a perfect specimen. Her bristly fur might be rough to the touch, but he'd never seen an ugly bear.

THIRTY-ONE

WESTON ROLLED TO ONE SIDE, adjusting to the discomfort of the first aid kit and his gun strapped beneath him. A late season mosquito hummed in his ear, receding and then gathering strength as it smelled blood. Next came the silence, then the bite, followed by a satisfying kill despite the sting.

Sleep came fast. So did the dream—except it wasn't a dream. It was for real. He walks to the edge of the river. He clutches the hand of the child. Who is this child? He's back in another life. Reeds hiss in the wind. At first he refuses to enter, but he relents and walks slowly into the river with the child. How far do they have to go? He wants to cross the river, needs to cross the river. He's desperate to cross the river. The path is unknown, boy in hand. He is blinded by the river, cannot see beneath its silver skin, sees with the painful soles of his feet coursing the jagged rocks blanketing the riverbed. It's a beginning, this pushing off from the edge of a shore that blows in and out from reality to dream. The reality is that he knows he's been here before. Everything is recognizable. Bumping against the shore, he feels braver, lightened much like the trees after an Alberta Clipper abates, branches abandoned from the weight of the storm. Behind him lies the river's perennial remains.

Suddenly, Matt appears, riding his motorcycle toward him, smiling defiantly as he speeds past him down the road.

"No, no!" Weston screams. "Stop—a car — "

Paralyzed, Weston can't wake himself from the image replaying itself as Matt appears and reappears over and over speeding down that gravel road, not looking, crossing the expressway into the path of an oncoming car.

Brand stood above Weston, shaking him, "Hey, wake up!"

Weston sat up. "What do you want?"

"You were screaming."

Weston stood up and looked at his watch. He hadn't slept long. "I'm okay." He stumbled over to check the fire. "What did I say?"

"'No—help'—crazy shit."

Brand looked a lot better, Weston thought, as he walked over to put a pot of water on the stove. "Looks like we need more wood."

Weston grabbed his coat, assuring his gun and first aid kit were secured to him before going outside. He'd have to be more careful now that Brand was recovering. It was very dark, and he had trouble following the path to the woodpile. Although the snow had lessened a little, there was no sign of a moon to light the way. If the storm didn't let up by tomorrow, he'd have to see what the river had to offer for food. He might catch a fish and boil cattail roots. He'd have to secure more dead wood to break up for the stove if they stayed much longer.

Brand was wide awake when he returned.

"You gonna' turn me in?"

"What do you think I should do?"

"I got this girl I want to marry."

"What's that got to do with anything? You've committed a crime. You escaped. You're a felon, a loser."

"I can't lose what I never had."

Weston wished he hadn't called him "a loser." He went to the stove and stoked it with wood, opened a can and stirred the stew. He doubted if he would ever be able to eat stew again in his life. "We may be more alike than we are different," Weston said beneath his breath.

"What did you say?"

"Nothing," Weston said. "I thought we'd hit the hay a couple of hours ago."

"Do you think there is something like stew poisoning?"

The light from the stove warmed the room. Exhausted as he was, Weston knew he couldn't sleep.

"Tell me about your kid," Brand blurted out as they ate the stew in the semi-darkness.

"He was a good kid."

"How old was he?"

"About your age."

"What happened to Kabakaba?" Brand asked.

"I'll tell you tomorrow. If this storm keeps raging, it'll be a long day. Better get some sleep."

THIRTY-TWO

THE WIND SOUNDED LESS FIERCE when Weston first woke and saw light through the window over Brand's cot. He shivered and drew himself down into his blanket. The bareness of the cabin with its raw board walls and rough-hewn floor made it feel colder. Maybe the storm was stopping, and cold weather had set in, as he knew was the case after a storm.

It had been a long time since he'd thought so hard on Chief Kabamappa. One day on their way to put in at the dam, he and Matt had stopped the truck to look down the river valley while driving the ridge along the St. Croix. An island overgrown with pine and underbrush stood midst the Northwood Flowage. "This was roughly where Kabamappa's village had been," he'd told Matt. "That was long before the CCC dam backed up the waters reducing what had been Kabamappa's settlement to a mere island." They tried to imagine what it had been like almost two hundred years ago. White Pines would have dominated the land. What puzzled Weston was how rapidly Kapamappa's world had disappeared, within a few decades. It was amazing to think that the Chippewas had lived the same way of life here for centuries. "Gone within forty years after the white men arrived," he'd told Matt. Today there was a sign pointing out Kabamappa's village right where he and Matt had stood contemplating the lost civilization. The sign said Kabamappa had signed the Treaty of 1837—seemingly a tribute to the Native American with no apology to Kabamappa's people for the resultant pillage.

Weston roused slowly, grimacing as his joints complained with each step. He needed to think seriously about early retirement. Brand was still asleep. The stove door clanked as Weston stoked it with wood. There were still a few coals. Weston groaned as he knelt to blow on the residue until he saw sparks emerge. Satisfied the wood would catch, he turned his thoughts to what was left on the shelf to eat. They needed more water to add to canned soup. He grabbed his coat and the snow pail.

What a relief to return to the river, his river. He scooped a pail full of snow near the water's edge. He'd have to boil the water if he took it from the river. Pure as it looked the St. Croix wasn't spring fed. He hated to return to the cabin. He'd spent his life concentrating on the past or imagining the future, but he was stuck in the moment, and it rubbed him the wrong way. He wanted to move forward in time, get out of the stench of wild bears, unwashed bodies and empty stew cans.

He wondered what Evie was up to alone in the house. Probably on the phone with her Spirit Club group. He shouldn't have been so short with her before he left. He'd have to spend more time with her, take her hunting and fishing. She'd gone with him and Matt a few times. He could tell she liked it. Maybe then she would talk to him about her finding her ancestors' spirits.

Brand was awake when he returned.

"So what happened to Kabakaba?"

"Kabamappa," Weston muttered. "Let me get some coffee and grub. My brain isn't awake yet."

By the time they'd eaten, and the fire was going full steam, Weston had to open the cabin door to cool the place off.

Noticing a let-up in the wind, he stuck his head out the screened porch door. If the storm stopped, Brand should be well enough to travel by tomorrow.

Weston checked Brand's arm, touching the area around the wound. "Looks better." He pulled a chair to the stove and sipped his coffee.

"Back to Kabamappa."

"What's that name mean?"

"The explorer, Nicollet, who came through the area with the Indian agent Schoolcraft translated it as 'He that sits to the side,' or as called by the whites, 'Wet Mouth.'"

"I don't get it."

"No one knows for sure. Maybe he chewed tobacco or always sat off to one side away from the others. Maybe he'd had a stroke, was weakened on one side and drooled. Who knows.

"In any event, he was friendly to the Indian agents that came through the area, helped them repair their canoes and gave them directions, according to the agents' reports. They described Kabamappa poling up the river standing in the bow of the canoe while his wife paddled in the stern. Kabamappa's clan wasn't always at that ancient Indian site you saw on the map. They moved around to stay ahead of the Sioux and find new hunting grounds. My grandpa always said they moved to stay ahead of the germs. They didn't have sanitation as we know it, and if they left the area for three weeks or so, the bed lice and parasites would die off."

"So what's so sad?" Brand asked.

"That's not the sad part. The sad part is what the white people and the American government did next. Let's see if I can remember how it went. Been a long time since I heard all this. It seems the white folks out east had run out of wood and needed to find new forests. You have to remember that there were no white people here in Wisconsin to speak of in the early eighteen hundreds and no towns. It was wilderness. There were no roads.

People traveled by footpaths or canoe. But what was here was very valuable. Do you know what that was?"

"What?"

"Trees, white pine trees that were hundreds of years old. Good solid lumber for houses and store buildings. Wisconsin wasn't a state yet, so the government had to claim the area as a territory and make it safe for white people to come in and log."

"What did Chief what's his face say about that?"

"He didn't have a lot to say. Actually, Indians were quiet people when they weren't conducting war parties or feasts. Anyway, the U.S. government gathered all the Chippewa chiefs together over near Minneapolis to get them to sign a treaty. It was 1837. Martin Van Buren was President of the United States. Kabamappa was there at the signing of the Treaty of 1837 and marked his X. The government asked the Indians for the white pines and the fur bearing animals, especially beavers. Beavers were valuable back then because Frenchmen bought them to make fur hats and such. In return for giving up the trees and animals, the Indians would be paid nine hundred thousand dollars along with blankets and whiskey and guns and pots and pans—but that was not so good for the Indians because they weren't used to alcohol."

"Sounds good to me, guns and hootch," Brand said.

"Sounded good to Kabamappa, too. However, the treaty said the money was to be paid over twenty years and that amounted to about seven dollars an Indian. Not too great when you figure it that way. Besides the guns were inferior. They often backfired and didn't always come with ammunition. But the worst of it was, the Indians couldn't read, and they really didn't know what they had signed. Many had too much to drink. Kabamappa literally caused his own downfall when he signed that treaty."

"They weren't too smart," Brand said.

"It wasn't that simple. They were smart enough all right— they knew how to survive in the wilderness and live off the land. They understood nature. But don't forget, they couldn't read. And they were dealing with Harvard educated lawyers and politicians. There was another problem the Indians faced. They didn't speak English. Their language was Ojibwa and because of the beaver trading with the French who came to the area from Canada they understood some French, but not English. They hadn't been exposed to it. It's hard to know what happened with the treaty after it was signed and taken back to Washington, but the documents must have been changed."

"How do you know that? You said you didn't know that much."

"Because of what took place on the St. Croix after the signing. Very soon, white people came in to log the territory. At first, the Indians weren't too upset because they still had access to the rivers, the land, and the wild rice fields in the area. That's what they thought the agreement had said. But then more and more white people began to settle the land, and with the threat of Indian warfare, especially between the Chippewas and the Sioux, the area became dangerous to the loggers and new settlers."

"So what happened around here?" Brand asked.

"Remember where the dam was that you had to go around?"

"Yeah, that's when the weather fucked up."

"During Kabamappa's time that was actually a natural beaver dam, so the water backed up causing a swampy area where the rice fields grew, but still left enough land for Kabamappa to grow potatoes, corn, and pumpkins. So this was a good place to have a village. They could fish for sturgeon in the swampy part they called Whitefish Lake. But when the loggers came they wanted the lake to store their cut timber, so they built a dam to raise the water level to create their log jam."

"The same one that's there now?"

"No, no. That's a modern dam now. Back then it was a log dam. When they wanted to send the logs downstream, they would remove the logs. That lowered the water level. Then they'd build it back up again and raise the water level to store their cut timber."

"So why would the Indian chief give a shit?"

Weston stopped and shook his head. "You know, Brand, we're going to have to work on your language. Your brain must be on overload with foul words."

"Sorry," Brand said.

"Kabamappa probably didn't care at first, but pretty soon it must have become apparent that the rice fields were being drowned and then dried out over and over, and the rice ultimately died out. Rising water gnawed away at the land, Kabamappa's land. That process surely would have ruined the fishing. The village would have been flooded over and over."

"Couldn't the Indians have stopped them?"

"Are you kidding? It was too late by the time they saw what was happening. They were nomadic people anyway and probably just moved on to another spot until that was overrun by more loggers and settlers. I don't know the particulars about that part. No Indians kept journals. I just surmise what had to have happened at Kabamappa's settlement."

"Shit," Brand said. "That's horrible."

"So you see, Chief Kabamappa caused his own demise when he signed that Treaty of 1837."

"Wonder why he would do it?" Brand said.

"Got a little greedy, I think."

Weston hadn't really figured out before now that Kabamappa had actually contributed to his own downfall until he said it aloud to Brand. Had Kabamappa's pride gotten the better of him? Blinded him to reality.

"I don't know if you've ever read any world history, but there's something else I don't understand."

"I'm just like the Indians," Brand said lowering his head. "I can't read very well."

"You can do something about that. The Indians couldn't. But what boggles my mind is that while for thousands of years other parts of the world had been writing and reading their own languages, the Chippewa people, right up to Chief Kabamappa's time, had no written Ojibwa language. They couldn't read or write. I wonder why they never developed that. Shows the importance of an education, doesn't it?"

Brand's eyes had glazed over, and Weston could tell Brand had lost interest in the Indian history lecture.

Weston rose to open the cabin door.

"Looks a little clearer out there. Want to walk down to the river with me?"

"Naw, you go ahead."

Weston pulled on his coat and pushed his way through the snow to the river. Talking about Kabamappa had depressed him. He hadn't wanted to discover that the famous Chippewa chief had been a party to his own demise. Weston thought a person ought be in control of his own life and that included the future.

At the river's edge, Weston calmed down. He hated to think about another night in the cabin that smelled more and more rotten by the hour. It looked as though they could set out tomorrow, though.

His mood improved with the prospect of leaving, and reaching down through the snow he grabbed hold of the canoe and lifted it to shake the snow loose.

Back in the cabin Weston couldn't resist saying, even though Brand seemed lost in a trance, "It doesn't seem that time heals all things after all, does it? Kabamappa would never have had enough time."

Brand stared up at a spider.

Weston couldn't figure if he'd even heard him. Maybe he was thinking about Kabamappa, dreaming of some long ago heritage. It would be tough to be a minority without a family to back you up. At least Matt and Evie had supportive relatives and ancestors they knew about. He didn't think Maria ever felt like an outcast. If anyone was the lone wolf in that clan, it was him.

Lying on his cot during the long days, Brand watched the spider at work. It hung out in the top corner of the window. At night it was silhouetted against the pale light from the window. It would have been long gone if they hadn't heated the cabin, but now heat had extended its work which was quite simple: to keep its web in repair, to catch food and stay alive. There probably wasn't much hope for trapping flying insects, but there might be a few crawlers left. He'd heard spiders eat other spiders. This one looked poisonous, big and black. Its web was secured delicately between the ceiling just below the roof line and the corner of the window. Because it was so high, there was no hope of wiping it clean, which would have been Brand's first move since it hung directly above his cot.

Periodically, the spider dropped vertically, suspending itself by a string of its web, looking him over. It probably considered him a spare refrigerator full of goodies, ready for the taking when its food supply ran low. Brand held his breath as the spider slowly descended, stopping just above his head, taunting him. He could have swatted and knocked it down, killed it at that point, but then there would have been nothing to watch. Besides it was a kind of thrill wondering whether it would stop. He would kill it in a minute if it landed on his body. Over the long hours, he'd learned plenty about the spider. It was very organized and spent a lot of time watching what was going on around. It took no chances. Safe in the cabin, it had no predators, except maybe Brand. It was very patient. Brand envied its haven.

Not as if Brand would know a safe place if he found one. He couldn't imagine what it was like to feel safe. Somebody would have to point it out to him—like hey, dumb-ass, you're safe here. He for sure wasn't safe here with a poisonous spider hanging over his head and a fucking prison warden at his side, both ready to strike at any given moment.

Brand had stopped taking the medication Weston was giving him. He held it in his cheek until Weston wasn't looking, then removed it and stashed it by the leg of his cot against the wall, not sure what his next move would be. One thing he had decided. He was going to suck up big time to Weston. What the shit. He had nothing to lose. Weston would probably kill him in the long run. He had never expected to live this long anyway.

"Want to hear about when I was a kid?"

Weston sighed, "I thought you were still a kid."

"I mean a little kid."

"Not really."

"Naw, I don't want to talk about being a kid. It was hell. I want to hear about you."

THIRTY-THREE

WESTON WASN'T SURE WHEN it happened, but he was losing his spunk to hate Brand. This had nothing to do with returning the prisoner to the authorities. He would still do that—that was his job. Maybe it was Brand's pluck to go it alone and escape, maybe the black eyes that burned into him. He couldn't understand his change of heart, and it bothered him.

"What do you want to know about me?" Weston finally said.

"You gonna' turn me in?"

"You asked me that before. Ask me something new."

"What's it like going without sex for so long?"

"You asked me that before, too." Weston hesitated. "Okay, it takes discipline."

Brand laughed.

"What's so funny?"

"Well, you know about discipline, all right."

That was good to hear. "Want to make something of yourself?" Weston finally asked.

"I got this girl I want to marry. She's part Indian, maybe related to that Chief."

"I doubt that. You told me about the girl before. You repeat yourself a lot." Weston pulled himself up to a sitting position, swinging his legs over the edge of the cot. "You interest me, Brand."

"No one ever said that to me."

"I'll bet they have, you probably didn't listen. But if you have a girl you want to marry, you have to get a job and all that. What direction do you want to go?"

Brand was quiet and Weston hoped he was thinking about that one.

"Maybe sideways?" Brand said.

The kid had a sense of humor.

"Want to know my motto?" Brand said.

"Sure."

"Take it and run."

"That figures," Weston said. "Tell me something, why did you want to escape? I know you won't tell me how, but I can't figure why."

"That's simple," Brand grinned. "Cause of you."

"Get off it."

"You rode me hard, and the inmates thought I was a snitch."

This was not what Weston wanted to hear, and he felt his anger surface. He knew he'd done the right thing. Brand was just too stupid to catch on.

"We'd better get some sleep. Maybe the storm will stop all together tomorrow, and we can head out."

Weston went outside for more wood, concerned about the scant pile out back. The snow was definitely lessening.

"Look," Brand said upon Weston's return. "I made you your coffee."

"That was thoughtful. Did you put sugar in it?"

Brand shook his head no, so Weston poured a slug directly from the bag into his cup.

"We better get some shut-eye. It could be a tough day tomorrow," Weston said as he downed the coffee in two big gulps.

When Weston woke it was just getting light, but all he could think about was the powerful pain in his head, pounding non-stop. He

172

couldn't remember falling asleep last night. He shut his eyes but couldn't lie still for the aching. Rousing himself enough to notice Brand under the covers, head and all, he decided to fall back to sleep until the headache was gone. When he woke next, it was cold in the cabin, but the pain was just as severe. There were still some coals in the stove, and he pushed at them until sparks rose before shoving in smaller pieces of wood. Brand was still asleep. He fell back on his cot and reached for his medicine kit to take something before his head split in two. He couldn't remember a headache like this in his life. Maybe he'd had a stroke. He lay still waiting for the pill to kick in. He felt his arms and legs for numbness in case it was a stroke. What in hell would he do out here with a wild prisoner if he couldn't move. The rest of him felt normal except for his damn head, so he quit worrying about a stroke and fell back to sleep.

He woke with a start and was confused because it was darker than when he woke up a little while ago. His head felt better but twice its normal size. He looked over at Brand and thought it odd that he was still in the same position.

"Hey, you die in your sleep?"

When Brand didn't answer, he forced himself up and shook Brand's shoulder only to find a wad of blanket, no Brand. Panicked, he pulled on his boots, grabbed his coat and raced out the cabin door. The canoes were still there pulled up on shore filled with snow, barely visible. It had stopped snowing and was almost dark. He must have slept all night and the next day. He couldn't believe it. He thought he was still dreaming and was going crazy. Running to the back of the cabin, Weston found the answer. There were Brand's footprints leading down the quarter mile path to the dirt road leading to County Road T. Brand lucked out. The bears had helped him escape by forging a path through the snow. Bears weren't dumb and obviously had used the path many times. They followed regular routes searching for food, preferring worn paths or roads rather than breaking through the brush.

Weston checked his medical kit. All the meds were still there. So was his gun. Brand had taken the garbage bag with his own stuff from under his cot.

How had Brand pulled it off? Weston felt like he'd been hit over the head but couldn't find a wound. One thing was for certain, Weston felt drugged and like a fool. Brand had done something no one had ever accomplished before. Brand had outsmarted him. He'd find him if it took the rest of his life.

Weston pulled on his sweater, coat and rain gear for extra warmth. Shaking his muddled head, he tried to figure out how to get out of here. Should he walk out like it looked that Brand had or should he canoe down to the next bridge? The next bridge took him farther away from the prison and his home. He'd be better off walking to T, hoping to thumb a ride. There were a few hunting cabins on T, but it was mainly all state-owned land. The corner gas station was several miles away. Walking out was still the best option. No chance of catching up with Brand. He was long gone. Once Weston reported the escape, Brand might be traced through hospitals. Surely, he'd have to end up at a hospital or somewhere in Milwaukee back on the streets.

THIRTY-FOUR

Brand wasn't at all sure he could do this, get himself up and out of here. He thought he'd go nuts waiting for Weston to fall into a deep sleep after slipping his meds into Weston's coffee. Maybe he'd made a mistake and should stick with Weston to get out of here, escape somewhere along the way. Weston had seemed sympathetic and might cut him a deal, but he knew better than to trust anyone in authority, or anyone at all, for that matter. Brand coughed a couple of times to see if Weston would respond. He even called to him, but Weston was knocked out.

He grabbed as many warm clothes as he could find, his garbage bag beneath the bed and spotted Weston's flashlight at the last minute. No way he was going to get in that canoe again and headed out behind the cabin. The snow had about ended. He stopped near the woodpile to put on more clothes and shined the flashlight around the yard, looking for bears and a way out to a road. Satisfied there were no bears, he couldn't believe his luck in finding a decent path through the snow and couldn't figure how it had been made. After plowing along for what seemed forever, he came to a small road and saw that the path through the snow continued to the left. It seemed logical that the road would follow the river. So he turned left, figuring it would lead him upstream. Finally it dawned on him that the bears had actually walked here. He was scared, but it was too late now to turn back.

A branch cracked in the forest. Brand jumped. Sure it was a bear, he shone his light toward the sound and saw a large black form that looked suspicious, but after studying it and finding it didn't move, decided it was shrub. The excitement kept him moving. His arm didn't even hurt. The going was slow. After an hour or so he was worried because he hadn't run into a larger road. There had to be one. There was no place to sit down and rest, but he had no time anyway. He wondered how long Weston would be out of it. Maybe he was already on his way after him. Brand had no idea how many pills he'd put in Weston's coffee. He'd grabbed all he'd saved over the days and hurriedly crushed them before dumping them in the mug along with a lot of sugar. Then Weston had added more sugar. Good thing Weston liked a lot of sugar.

It was so quiet out here, almost peaceful if he wasn't so desperate to escape. Even though limbs snapped from trees, he couldn't hear them fall. He no longer jumped thinking they were gun shots.

He couldn't stop picturing the girl. She'd remember him all right, but would she be waiting for him? She'd have to be home because it was night. He remembered her saying something about her old man. Maybe he was home. Probably asleep. He wasn't even sure he'd know her house from the road, but he'd worry about all that when he got there.

After what seemed like another hour, a partially plowed road surfaced. Not sure which direction to take, he decided to stay on the right hand side of the river, so he turned that way. But then he wondered if he was making a mistake. Maybe he should go the other way and avoid Northwood. That might be safer. What the fuck, he thought, it's the girl I want.

Walking was easier now. He relaxed a little given the chance a car might come along. As long as it wasn't a sheriff. He figured it wasn't quite midnight yet. It was too wild out here, though. He missed the city clutter. He preferred city muck where he could disappear in the alleys. Out here he was too aware of himself.

There must have been a forest fire a while back because now all he could see were remnants of trees along the road. Their black spikes were eerie as though he were walking through a horror movie. He'd been in a fire once, and remembered running outside to the street. He watched smoke turn from white to black, billowing from windows and holes in the roof. It'd given him a hard on. He'd seen a couple of fires since then, and it always had the same effect.

A couple of times he thought he heard a car, but it never came any closer. It wasn't horribly cold, and there wasn't much wind. He heard it again, and this time he was sure it was a car. Lights appeared. He didn't know what to do so he stopped and put out his thumb. It passed him right by. Brand shook his good arm at the car and swore at the driver as he was left in a swirl of exhaust-filled snow.

He was depressed as he dragged himself along the road. If he had to, he would walk all the way to Northwood, but he had no idea how far it was or how long it would take him. After all he'd been through, he figured could stand anything.

Actually, Weston wasn't a bad cop, Brand thought, just a dumb cop. He could have let him die or killed him and no one would have known. He knew Weston had a good reputation. It hadn't taken as long as he'd thought to soften Weston's tough gut. He was surprised it had been so easy. All along Weston had hated him, and Brand couldn't figure why, but he knew how to suck people in. He'd learned it the hard way in prison. The lesson was simple: con or be conned.

One time he'd talked a prison secretary into getting him drugs. He'd started slow, asking for a pencil at first. Prison workers weren't allowed to give even a piece of paper to an inmate. So all he'd had to do was find out something personal about her and work on that. He'd overheard her on the phone saying her sister had just had a baby, and it wasn't normal. So the next day he came to tell her he'd just heard from his mother that she'd had another baby and its spinal cord was hanging out of its backside. The secretary seemed sorry for him. So he asked for paper and pen to write his mom. One request led to another and then he asked for the drugs. She said, "No," at first, said she'd be fired for that, and she needed her job. So he told her he was going to report her for all the other stuff she'd given him, and she'd be fired for that. She delivered the drugs. It was called the sting.

An engine roared behind him. A snowplow crawled through banks of flying snow. Brand hailed the driver explaining he'd been caught in the storm and had holed up in a cabin on the river. The driver waved him into the cab.

"Going to Northwood?" Brand yelled over the noise.

"Might take a while, but you're welcome to ride along."

It was better than nothing, and no one would think to look for him in a snowplow even if Weston had roused himself by now.

The snowplow driver was too busy to talk so Brand leaned his head back in the seat and slipped into semi-sleep lulled by the drone of the plow. He was back in the snow cave waiting to be eaten alive, wanting to die, a cold place that was keeping him warm. He was apart from his body in a kind of no-self state, feeling no pain, seeing himself from a distance, very much in the cave. He'd lost his identity, and it felt good to be no one.

The plow jerked him awake, but he closed his eyes again and willed himself back to la-la land where he wasn't a fugitive. He'd managed to hypnotize himself even without the drugs. He'd have to try this more often. It was cool. Just close his eyes and imagine himself back in his cave, scared shitless—yet feeling so safe.

Next thing he knew the snow plow driver was shaking him by the shoulder.

"I have to let you off here. I can't go off my route."

"Where am I?"

"We're right at Highway 53 and County Y. Just walk straight ahead. This is Northwood."

"Where's the river?"

"Straight ahead. This road crosses the Eau Claire River."

Brand rolled out of the cab, still half asleep, elated to think he'd gotten this far. He'd gone past the St. Croix and was back to where he started, well, almost. Walking toward the river, he recognized the Buckhorn Tavern although he'd never gotten beyond the front entrance, thanks to Ryder, and then passed the road that he remembered led into the baseball park. He knew enough to turn up river on the road just before the bridge and thought it couldn't be too far from here. The cold air cleared his head but wasn't enough to really wake him up and feel good. He couldn't remember feeling this tired. His arm ached to the top of his head. He tried to distract himself from the pain. It wouldn't be long until he saw the girl. He would touch her, hold her, fuck her.

He wished he'd counted how many houses he'd passed after the girl's when he was on the river. The water had been too fast, but it couldn't be more than a mile or two. He could only walk so fast now, no strength left. He passed about five places and then turned in a drive to see if he recognized the house, but quickly realized this wasn't it. It was a junk heap. Her place had been neat and clean. He walked past the next drive and turned down the one after that, but that wasn't it either. He couldn't stop now. He'd have to keep going until he dropped. He had nowhere else to go, except to let the fucking sheriff find him in a heap beside the road. After two more attempts, he finally dragged himself into a drive that he thought looked familiar. He remembered there was a barn past the house toward the river, but it was still dark enough that he couldn't see. He almost gave up hope of finding her before remembering it was still late at night, almost morning in fact. She'd be here asleep.

He knocked on the back screen door, then opened it and knocked on the closed door. He tried the knob, and it was locked. There was no sound inside. After knocking louder, he decided to throw pine cones at the upstair's window. Finally a light came on, and he heard footsteps on the stairs. He prayed it wasn't her old man and stood off to the side.

Opening the door a slit, Evie peered out.

"Hi, it's me. I'm back," he whispered.

She pulled him inside. "I can't believe it." She pulled him inside. "You're hurt. They didn't catch you?"

"Sort of," and with a burst of energy, he pulled her to him with his good arm.

"I am so glad to see you." She held him at arm's length. "But what happened to your arm?"

"Where's your dad? You said you had a dad."

She guided him into the living room where Brand collapsed in a chair.

She knelt before him. "He's not home. What happened? You're sick. You need to lie down."

"Not yet. I have to kiss you," but he couldn't muster the energy to even lean forward. "Can we lie down somewhere?"

"Sure, come up to my room."

Brand grabbed her with his good arm and kissed her hard on the mouth.

"But you can't stay long. We have to get you out of here soon," Evie said. "You need some rest and something to eat. You look awful. Does it hurt? Don't worry, I've got a car."

"Oh, Baby," and he slumped into a chair. "I am so fucking tired—something for the pain."

Evie helped him up, and he followed her up the stairs.

THIRTY-FIVE

IT TOOK LONGER THAN WESTON had expected to fight his
way through the snow to reach Highway T. He felt so help-
less following in Brand's footsteps, drawn along by an escapee,
dragged by an invisible rope. On the other hand, maybe Brand
had collapsed somewhere along the road, and Weston would
stumble across him.

Weston was dressed way too warm, and sweat streamed down
his chest. The exercise helped to clear his head. The snow had
stopped, but it was getting darker. He had looked around the
cabin for his flashlight but couldn't find it. Brand must have
taken it. Brand, the mere thought made Weston see red. He'd
thought he was beginning to see hopeful signs in Brand, rehabilitation perhaps. But Brand had conned him. Weston hated to
admit it or even think of the possibility. Throughout his career,
no one had ever done a con job on him. A few had tried and
learned to regret it.

Clouds still shrouded the stars. He'd forgotten the moon's
cycle. It could be full for all he knew. He wondered how long it
would take him to reach a phone.

The dirt road was rutted, layered with deep snow, hard to
maneuver. The bears had walked here, too, and so had Brand.

Weston shifted his pack to his other shoulder and wondered how far Brand had gotten and where he was headed. Probably back to Milwaukee. They all headed for home. Brand had said he had no family left there, but who could believe the liar. He'd even admitted to being a liar. It was a long hike to Milwaukee, but he'd had a good night and day's head start. Brand must have picked up a ride, easy to find a sympathetic sucker in this weather. He was too weak to have walked very far.

Weston wondered what Ryder was thinking. Maybe they'd picked up Brand, and he'd told them where Weston was. Naw, Brand was too much of a rat to help anyone but himself. Weston hadn't remembered how long this road was out to T. He stopped to catch his breath. He'd usually arrived at the cabin by canoe.

He continued to worry about Evie and hoped she was smart enough to stay home until the snow had stopped. He hoped she remembered to feed Precious. She was probably pretty worried about him. Until the last few months, she'd been mothering him — that is, until she got into that Indian spirit thing that galled him. He wished he'd hung around the ricing ritual more. Maybe he would have learned how they invoked spirits to reap a good crop and all that stuff. He didn't think they actually danced around the fire in a religious fashion, but his wife had talked about dancing while shaking husks from the grain. Anyway, he never concerned himself with communing with dead spirits like Evie was doing. He was ashamed to talk to anyone such as the minister or her teachers about her foolishness. He'd put an end to it when he got home.

Weston felt tired and old. He looked at the silhouettes of drooping trees. The brittle limbs had succumbed to the storm, and remaining branches hung low supported by the snow on the ground but they would snap back once the snow melted. Maybe he should retire right away before everyone said he'd lost his touch. It would be hard to uphold his reputation and keep order in the prison after this. How could he look an inmate in the eye and demand respect after he'd allowed one to con him.

When he finally reached County T, Weston was exhausted. His head pounded with each step, and he fumbled in his pack for aspirin. If only a car would come by. He looked to the west, but saw nothing.

The St. Croix was a couple hundred yards west. He heard its water rushing beneath the bridge. It called to him, and he longed to go to the river but couldn't take the time. He knew the effect that gazing into the black water whether churning or quietly deep had on him. Solace would wrap round him and hold him secure. The world would stop; eternity would prevail. A full moon had somewhat the same effect but not nearly as profound as the river that held him captive.

Turning east on T, he trudged forward. The road had been plowed in one lane, so cars would be traveling slowly. He figured it was about eight or nine P.M., but it could be later. Surely someone would drive by. Those young pickup truck guys were always on the move at odd hours.

For a while back there in the cabin, Weston had flirted with recommending a light reprimand as punishment for escaping, such as an extra year, a sentence Weston could monitor. But not after this. Brand was in for it now. Weston could hardly wait until they found him. It was back to maximum if Weston had any say. So what if Brand had been subject to prison rape. If he was so smart, let him con the cons from here on.

Weston couldn't imagine an inmate not taking advantage of a good opportunity, but he'd seen it fail time after time. Inmates were hard wired to think for the moment, unable to imagine the future, let alone accept consequences for their actions. On top of that, they were completely self-centered, no feelings for others or caring how they felt.

Weston heaved a sigh. No point in using up his energy on frustration. He concentrated on placing one foot in front of the other, willing the pain in his head to disappear.

He had no idea how much time had passed and thought he was dreaming when he heard the drone of a car engine in the distance and stopped to listen. The wind had picked up. It was coming from the west and behind him. Headlights appeared around the corner as a truck crossed the St. Croix bridge and barreled toward him spraying snow over the top of the cab.

Stepping into the middle of the road, he wildly flailed his arms and yelled, "Help! help! — I need help!" praying it wouldn't run him down.

The truck spun to a stop. A young kid rolled down the window

"For Christ's sake, you crazy? I almost ran you down."

"Can I bum a ride?"

There were two other teenagers in the front seat of the pickup. "I guess we can squeeze you in. Where you headed?"

"Northwood."

"You in a hurry? We got a couple of stops."

Weston smelled liquor and could guess what the stops were. "I'm in kind of a hurry, but I'm grateful for the ride."

"Some storm. You get caught in it?"

"Yeah, I was on the river."

"I was too little to remember the last Clipper. You seen many?"

"Seen my share."

The kid drove more slowly with Weston in the car. They rode in silence for awhile until lights from the Corner Store gas station came into view.

"Gotta make a quick stop here," and he swung the truck into the only plowed space.

"Mind if I make a phone call?" Weston asked. "Want to reassure my family."

The kids disappeared to the liquor section. Weston dialed the prison first. Ryder wasn't there, and Weston decided not to explain anything to the night guard on phone duty. He called Ryder's house, but no one answered, then called his own house.

He let the phone ring several times, but no one was home there either. Puzzled that the answering machine didn't click on, he was distracted watching the boys showing their ID as they paid for the beer, relieved he didn't have to get into that and went out to the truck, anxious to get going.

"I guess I'll have you drop me off at my place, if you don't mind," Weston said.

About thirty minutes later they pulled up to his drive.

"Thanks for the lift," Weston said and couldn't resist adding, "Be careful out there." They waved in return, and he turned to walk down the drive, trees on either side bent low to the ground with their burden. Except for the oaks. They held up on their own, no bending or swaying. Instead, they would crack under pressure. He pushed his way through the snow toward the house, pleased that someone had been here to plow the drive. Everyone around here had a plow on the front of their truck. Could have been anyone. A light in the kitchen meant Evie had to be home. He wondered why she'd leave a light on unless maybe she was scared. He'd taught her to be cautious. Comforting ice crystals hung from pine needles glittering next to the kitchen window as though to welcome him. Funny the things that eased your mind, he thought.

About to enter the back door, Weston noticed the barn door was wide open and went to close it. His instincts told him he should be racing into the house to check on Evie, call the sheriff's office, the prison, find Ryder, but life had lost its urgency. He'd fought to exhaustion the voices within him questioning how he could have allowed the past sweep of events, letting Brand get away.

He flicked on the barn light when he couldn't find Precious in her stall. She was gone, escaped. He looked around the outside of the barn and found deer tracks leading toward the river. It looked like more than one deer. He didn't have the time or strength to track her now.

He'd been afraid she would escape someday but not during an Alberta Clipper. His heart sank thinking he might never see her again. Maybe she'd find her way home if she survived that long. Not likely she would know her way through a forest she'd never known.

Turning off the barn light, he headed for the house.

THIRTY-SIX

Evie had a thousand questions to ask, but knew better than to press Brand right now.

"Here's my room. Lie down and sleep for a couple of hours. We have to get you out of here as soon as possible."

"So how will you get me out of here?"

"I told you I have a car. I can drive you to the Canadian border."

She turned the light on in her room. He turned it off and pulled her to him.

"No, you don't understand. You must rest and then we will leave."

"But you said you loved me in your note."

"So?"

"I know what that means."

"Okay, okay, lie down."

Brand started to take off his pants.

"Keep your clothes on."

Before she knew it, Brand was asleep. She went down to kitchen to make him something to eat. He must be starving. No wonder he looked so tired.

By the time she came back upstairs, Brand was in a sweat. She felt his burning forehead. She'd have to let him rest a few hours. She'd have to risk her father coming home before they could leave. She was down in the kitchen when she heard him call her.

"Hey, Baby."

Gathering the food she'd prepared, she found some aspirin and hoped he was better as she went up to him in her room.

She put down her armful and leaned over to feel his forehead. Brand grabbed her arm and threw her on the bed.

"Hang on," Evie yelled at him. "This is my house. You need to mind me, you jerk."

"You're right. Okay, what's up?"

"Well, I guess you're better, right?"

Brand devoured the food, then laid back and shut his eyes. "I am so tired."

They stretched out on the bed, Evie moving to the far side. She reached over to hold his hand.

"Now, let me explain. I can drive you to the Canadian border—with me along you can make it across."

"So why are doing this, you crazy or something—risking your life—for me?"

"Like, here's the story. I had a brother. He was killed in a motorcycle accident. He was your age. Like, we were both half-Indian, just like you. It happens that for some odd reason, except I think it is a plan, that you look like my brother, Matt—in fact, you look exactly like him."

Brand threw his hand over his forehead. "Shit, I thought it was love at first sight. Now I find out I'm your dead brother."

"It's something like that—only more. I believe in dead spirits living on. My brother lives on in you."

He bolted upright in bed. "I'm out of here."

"Okay—where are you going, smart Indian boy?"

"Evie leaned over and kissed Brand on the forehead. He grabbed her, and suddenly Evie discovered how good it felt to be in this wild Indian man's arms. She wanted him for life.

Afterward, she was disappointed that Brand hadn't been as kind with her as she had hoped. He's been deprived too long, she thought. Brand fell asleep instantly.

Evie clung to the hope that she could reform this crazy young Indian who looked just like Matt. It was her mission. His return to her was proof he possessed Matt's spirit. Her dad had never understood how much she needed her mother's Indian connection, and she resented that. He was all about rules and control, never understood her inner spirit, or Matt's, for that matter. She was sure Matt had played that stupid chicken game in defiance of his father's control. Sometimes she hated her father.

She needed to get them up, though, get dressed and on their way. She'd just close her eyes for a minute.

In the back of the dream she was having, where they were being chased by the police while driving to the border, she heard a door slam. It wasn't enough to fully wake her.

THIRTY-SEVEN

SEATED AT A TABLE IN THE bare courtroom, Weston stares straight ahead, past Judge Pearson, seeing nothing, fading in and out of the proceedings. Those behind him, those who have come to see the fiasco, sit quietly. They must be holding their breath, he thinks, gloating over sealing my fate. Fate? His grandpa had always said when something happened that was out of his control, "It's the fate of the gods, just like the Greek said," as though one Greek knew all the answers. The only Greek Weston could recall was a salesman who came to Northwood once a year in springtime, the rear of his car sagging with an overload of perfume and soaps. He remembers his grandpa as old, uneducated and toothless. What did he know about ancient Greeks except to twist a saying to fit the occasion.

Weston doesn't believe in fate anyway, now that he thinks about it. Fate means no control, and he'd always believed in absolute control. So how did he get here, in front of a judge to judge him. Who was to blame? For one thing, the relaxed prison codes are to blame by preventing him from doing his job properly, and he blames Brand. Here he is hating Brand again just when he'd started to like him.

Had his grandpa's gods brought him down, stolen his pride? "Find your own Olympus," his grandpa had said. Maybe the old

190

man had studied the Greeks after all. Not too long ago, Weston thought he'd found his Olympus, fought his way to the top. He'd been there a long time when without any warning he slipped down the rocky slope. Now here he is wallowing in Hades. He's thankful his grandpa or his dad, for that matter, aren't here to watch.

His lawyer is young enough to be his son, too young for Weston to trust. Weston couldn't stand the thought of a trial, didn't want his peers to judge him. The young lawyer hadn't agreed at first, but Weston reminded him who was paying whom, so he went along with relying on the fairness of a judge, and as it happened, a fair judge had been assigned to his case. Weston had cooperated with law enforcement. That's in his favor, he thinks, plus the fact he'd turned himself in. The prosecution's lawyer is making him out to be a demented criminal. In fact, Weston's lawyer even suggested at first that they plea temporary insanity. Weston was appalled and would have none of it. He knew what he was doing. He may have committed a crime in the eyes of the law, but he is no criminal.

Judge Pearson is asking him a question. "Did Jeffrey Brand threaten you?"

"No, sir," Weston murmurs.

"Speak up, Mr. Weston."

He knows he's tuning out but can't help himself. He needs time to think. Then all this might make sense to him.

"Mr. Weston, can you hear me?" Judge Pearson asks, leaning toward the defendant.

Weston's lawyer turns to him. "You need to answer."

Weston tries to clear his brain. "Yes, Your Honor."

The prosecuting attorney moves to the front of the court-room. "Tell us exactly what happened when you returned home."

Weston sees the words form in the attorney's mouth before he hears them. What happened when I returned home, Weston repeats to himself.

"Do you need a recess, Mr. Weston?" Judge Pearson interrupts.

"No, your honor, I think I can explain."

No need to tell about not finding Precious, Weston thinks before he speaks, "I opened the back door. The kitchen light was on. There was no sound so I assumed Evie was asleep. I called the prison and again reached the phone guard."

"What do you mean by 'again'?" the prosecution begins.

Weston tries not to react defensively. He knows it will do no good, but he can't help taking affront at the prosecuting attorney's attitude. Why isn't he wearing a coat and tie, for God's sake? Who does he think he is—not representing the state with respect? He watches as the attorney slouches toward him.

Weston's not going to play that game and aims to sound calm and professional. "I had called from the Corner Store gas station to see if Brand had been apprehended and decided not to bother explaining my situation until I got home. After calling the prison from my house, I dialed the sheriff's office to learn Brand had not been captured, and they had no lead as to his whereabouts. I called Ryder and woke him up. I explained the situation in detail and asked him to call the sheriff and explain what had happened concerning me because I was too exhausted to go through it all again. We decided I should get some sleep."

"And did you go to bed, Mr. Weston?" the prosecutor asks turning dramatically toward Judge Pearson.

"I poured myself a glass of milk and took it upstairs."

"Did you go directly to your bedroom?" the lawyer spins around and demands.

"I had to pass Evie's room, and I looked in to make sure she was all right. I turned on the hall light so I could see better."

"And . . ." the attorney waves both hands toward himself forcing a rapid response.

Weston waits before answering, "Something seemed odd so I called to her."

"What seemed odd to you?"

"She wasn't on the side of the bed she usually sleeps on."

"And what happened when you called to her?"

Weston pauses. The questions are coming too fast. He takes a deep breath and says, "She screamed."

"Then what did you do?"

"I reached in her room and turned on the light."

"And what did you find?" the prosecutor demands.

Once again Weston stops and looks down at his feet.

"Mr. Weston? Did you understand the question?" Judge Pearson asks.

"Yes, Your Honor. She was in bed with a man." He can't bring himself to say they were nude.

"Did you speak to her?" the prosecuting attorney cuts in.

Weston tries to remain calm. The attorney is proceeding too fast. He wishes he could respond directly to the judge.

"'Evie,' I said. 'What are you doing? Who is this man?'"

"Then what?"

Weston heaves a sigh. "They sat up, and I saw who it was."

The prosecutor moves closer to Weston and hisses in his face, "Did you know this man?"

"Yes, it was Jeffrey Brand, the inmate that had escaped from prison, the same inmate I had captured on the river, nursed back to health in the fishing cabin on the river, who had drugged me and escaped from the cabin."

Once again the prosecutor dramatically turns his back on Weston and asks, "What did you do then?"

Weston waits until the prosecutor faces him. He refuses to speak to someone's back.

"Your Honor," Weston says. "I do not understand why the prosecuting attorney asks me a question and then turns his back on me."

Judge Pearson beckons the prosecutor to the bench.

"I apologize," the prosecutor says returning to Weston, then asks the court reporter to repeat the question.

"And what did you do then?" the court reporter reads.

Weston continues, "I almost collapsed in shock. I couldn't stand to look so I turned from the room and went back downstairs."

"Is that all you did? Didn't you call the sheriff?" The prosecutor speaks more softly.

"No, I sank into the living room chair and hid my face in my hands. Tears ran down my face. I couldn't stop until I heard Evie and Brand coming down the stairs. They were arguing."

"What were they saying?"

"Brand was yelling at Evie, 'Why didn't you tell me your father was . . . '

"'Shut up,' Evie said.

"'We gotta get out of here,' Brand told her."

"And what did you do then?"

"I grabbed my gun."

"Did Brand try to hit you, hurt you?"

"No, he kept his arm around Evie. I couldn't stand the sight of them."

Weston drops his head in his hand and turns away from the bench.

"Did you want to hurt them or kill them?" the prosecutor asks.

Weston can't bring himself to speak. He'd always thought an image was as much a part of reality as the hard truth. It's also why he'd resisted a trial. He would rather die than say what he knows he has to say now, not only under oath, but in front of everyone. Sweat breaks out on his forehead, and he waits as it runs down his neck to his chest. He pulls out his handkerchief to calm himself, stalling for time.

"Are you all right, Mr. Weston?" Judge Pearson asks.

Weston's lawyer stands up to respond.

Weston looks at his lawyer, clears his throat and says, "I can go on."

"I'll repeat the question," the prosecutor says. "Did you want to hurt them?"

"They betrayed me," Weston murmurs.

"Speak up, Mr. Weston."

Weston lifts his head and bellows to the rafters, "I wanted to kill Brand!" His words reverberate against the wooden walls.

Gasps emerge from the audience. The judge pounds his gavel. "Order!"

The prosecutor leans toward Weston. "Mr. Weston, think carefully, at any time did Mr. Brand threaten you with words or by force?"

"No, he did not."

"What did you say to them?"

This is harder than Weston had ever imagined. "I remember saying to Evie, 'So you are the so-called girlfriend!'"

"What did she do?"

"All the time Brand was trying to drag her out the door, yelling, 'We gotta' get out of here. He's going to shoot me.'"

"What did your daughter do?"

"She resisted Brand and said, 'Put down the gun, Dad.' She sounded so calm. They started for . . ."

Weston stops in mid-sentence, suddenly confused and befuddled. It is late in the afternoon. He needs time to rethink what happened, sort it out step by step.

He whispers to his lawyer.

"My client is exhausted and not well. We'd like to request a recess until tomorrow."

"Granted," says the judge.

The next morning when Weston is back in the courtroom, he thinks he's sorted out what happened and is ready to finish the tale of his downfall. He will repeat it exactly as he told it to Ryder.

THIRTY-EIGHT

THINKING BACK ON THE HORROR of what had happened,
Weston had stumbled to the phone and called Ryder. "You
better get over here," he gasped.

Still holding the gun, Weston dragged himself out to the
barn. Everything inside him had died. He felt like a fish that had
been gutted. There was no anger or hate left. Life had checked
out on him.

Once he'd read that progress took forever, destruction but a
second. It was a horrible thought, but at this point it was the
only truth he could believe in. He looked down at the gun in his
hand as though someone else held it. He could end it all now.
Take only a second. But those were the thoughts of a coward,
and he put his gun back in its holster.

From habit, he looked to the barn, noticed the yard light
was on and like a robot, headed outside. He spotted where
Precious had pranced around and flattened the snow, then
noticed larger hoof prints in the same area. He followed her
path to the river until it was too dark to see. Big buck, Weston
thought, but couldn't muster the energy to follow the tracks any
farther. Still in a fog, he plodded back to the barn and looked
inside. He thought he saw movement, maybe an animal eating
Precious' corn, so he walked inside. There was Precious in her

stall sniffing about for something to eat. She'd overturned her empty grain pail.

A flicker of relief flashed through him, and he stretched out his hand to rub her muzzle.

"Decided to come back home, did you?"

"What are you doing out here?" Ryder startled Weston.

"Better come in the house," Weston said.

Weston sat at the kitchen table and put his head in his hands.

"Well, what's so important to get me out of bed before daylight?" Ryder grumbled.

"You won't believe this," Weston began, summoning the strength to explain how he'd found Brand in Evie's bed. "Sit down, Ryder."

"Where are they? You didn't shoot him, did you?"

"The son-of-bitch. It seems Evie had helped him escape. They'd been writing notes to each other all along. He deserved to be shot!"

Ryder looked about the room before taking a seat. "Tell me exactly how it happened."

"I had come down to the living room." Weston choked up and waited to collect himself. "I was so devastated and ashamed, ashamed of Evie, ashamed myself. I'd been duped! All that time I'd spent nursing him back to health in the cabin. Should have let him die. I almost began to like him, reminded me so much of Matt. Then Evie and Brand came into the living room, Brand pulling Evie along.

"I took one look at them and started yelling. I don't know what came over me. 'Get out of here. Get out of my sight!' I screamed. Over and over I yelled, 'Get out! Get out!' Maybe I was afraid I was going to shoot him." Weston choked up and turned his face away to collect himself.

"Then Brand said, 'Come on, let's get out of here. He's got a gun.' He pulled Evie along and headed for the door.

"Evie grabbed her car keys and a bag she apparently had packed earlier. How could they have planned all this behind my back?"

Weston stopped to wipe the sweat pouring down his forehead.

"So that was it? You didn't shoot Brand? You let him escape?"

"Let him? Didn't you hear me? My last words were, 'Go! Get out of my sight!'"

"Excuse me, Carl, but thank God you didn't shoot him." Ryder shook his head. "Wait a minute. Back up and tell me how you caught him."

Weston leaned back in his chair and went through the whole scenario from capture to Brand's escape and then finding them together in his home.

"I can't believe this," Ryder said when Weston had finished.

"Well, you better believe it." Weston leaned across the table and grabbed Ryder by the hands. "Take me in, Ryder," Weston begged. "I should have slapped handcuffs on Brand right then and there. I lost it! I am a criminal!" Weston sobbed. "The award-winning prison superintendent committed the worst imaginable crime. I let, no! I helped an inmate escape!"

"Now wait a minute, Carl. No one knows about this. You were the professional you were trained to be, capturing him under the worst circumstances, then taking care of him and nursing him back to health. You performed your duty to the letter. You could have come home, found them, and Brand forced you to let them go. It would be your word against Brand."

Weston stared Ryder in the eye. "I can't believe you said that, Ryder." Weston leaned onto the table toward Ryder. "Come on, Ryder. Who are you kidding? You know, Evie knows, Brand knows, and the God deep in here knows," Weston said, pounding his chest.

Ryder looked away. "I can't believe I said that either."

"It's the law, Ryder. We've got to have laws! We've got to control things!" He covered his eyes. "What do I know? I lost control. The worst of it is—I don't know how I let it happen. I didn't plan it." Weston bent over, cradling himself. "Tell me, Ryder, why did I do this?"

"Let's get some sleep, Carl. I will put out an alarm right now to pick up Evie and Brand. Do you have any idea where they went?"

"I figure they headed for Canada. They'll get picked up soon enough. I want Evie to come back on her own. Brand is not dangerous. He doesn't have a gun."

"Go on upstairs. I'll stay the night here."

Weston struggled to rise and lumbered up the stairs.

THIRTY-NINE

DURING THE LAST WEEK while waiting for his sentencing, Weston had walked the woods, avoided people, cared for Precious and worried about Evie. He should never have kicked her out but knew she would have run away with Brand no matter what he'd said. At night he'd wake in a sweat having dreamt he heard her scream, "I'm never coming back."

He wondered if his disgrace would be announced in the weekly Shopper. Excused on his own cognizance, he was not required to post bond. His lawyer and Ryder had suggested plea-bargaining, but Weston considered that a cop out.

One day, Weston stopped to pick up his mail at the post office, hoping for word from Evie. The postmistress was closing for her lunch break. "Come on in, Carl," Sally said. "I'm in no rush."

He was disappointed to find no message from Evie although he knew he shouldn't expect to hear from her after the way he'd thrown her out of the house. Now he wished he had it to do over again. He'd clap handcuffs on Brand before he knew what hit him. Evie would get over it.

Sally grabbed her leather jacket, followed him out the door and locked up to go to lunch. "Why don't you join me at the Buckhorn?"

Sally was native to Northwood same as he and had her share

of troubles, too. Her daughter was in school with Evie, but she wasn't into that Indian spirit thing. Then again, Sally's daughter had no Indian blood. In addition to sorting mail behind her counter that supported a massive scales, Sally served as confessor to many. She had a motherly air about her that invited conversation. Maybe it was her round pretty face, devoid of make-up, that spoke to her sincerity. He probably should have talked to Sally earlier about Evie's strange Resurgence of Spirit interest. Too late now.

"Winter's here early," he said.

"I'll be there at the sentencing," she said right off.

"Don't bother." Weston looked away, pleased to see the Buckhorn was practically empty.

"I hope you don't go to jail. That wouldn't be fair."

"What's fair?" Weston asked, turning to face her, "Nothing's fair."

Sally shrugged, toying with her glass of water.

"If I'd operated on *fairness*, I'd have been fired long ago," Weston said. "Keeping order is what it's all about."

Debby appeared to wait on them looking rather sullen. Weston ordered a hamburger and fries. She didn't pay much attention to him. He smiled up at her, and started to say he liked her new blond hairdo, but she was already on her way back to the kitchen. Weston felt hurt at her rejection.

"What do you hear from your boy?" Weston asked.

"He's due home on a leave soon."

"Better than Iraq."

"Thank goodness, but I've got two nephews over there," Sally said.

Weston wondered if Matt would have enlisted. He probably would have signed up against Weston's will, if for no other reason than to defy him.

Debby reappeared with their meals. Normally, Weston would have given her a friendly pat on the back and joked with her about looking too pretty for her own good. But not today. She avoided Weston like a skunk at the back door, reaching all the way across the table to serve him his food instead of walking around.

"How's your soup? Smells good," Weston asked Sally, leaning forward to sniff it.

"Umm, they do make good chicken soup, make the stock from scratch."

Pete came in for his noon beer and waved to them, but acknowledged only Sally. Weston called out to him anyway. He could have tipped his cap to me, Weston thought, annoyed by the lack of respect. Winter and summer, Pete wore a baseball cap with a Packers logo emblazoned across the front. Weston figured Pete was covering for a lack of hair, but he wasn't sure because he never saw him without that damn cap. Who cares about a thing like hair anyway, Weston thought. He had sported a bald spot for years, and it never bothered him, anyway not enough to wear a hat year in and year out.

"This all happened so fast, Carl, before rumors could circulate," Sally said, ignoring Pete. "How did you manage that?"

"Looks like the word's out anyway," nodding toward Pete. "First of all, I turned myself in to the sheriff right away. Ryder went with me the next morning. And I chose not to have a jury trial. That sped up the process a lot."

Sally broke open a roll but rejected the butter Weston offered. "You on a diet?" Weston asked.

"Sort of. What are you going to do, Carl, after this is over?"

"Probably go to jail."

Sally laughed. "I doubt that."

"Well, after jail time, I'll come right back to the Eau Claire and live off the river."

"I'll be right here to welcome you."

"Where else would I go? The moon or Mars? This is my world."

Sally looked at her watch and rose to go back to work. "I'll be there supporting you at the sentencing."

He guessed the weekly Shopper would be on to it. He'd been right thinking everyone sitting behind him had been against him. Well, maybe not everybody. There was always Sally. But then what did he know anymore? Obviously, Debby wasn't supporting him. And he sure couldn't count on Pete. Weston was relieved Sally hadn't asked about Evie. He picked up his package of mail and walked over to the bar to pay, but Sally had already paid his bill.

Debby avoided looking him in the eye.

"See you around, Debby," Weston said.

She was already back in the kitchen and never answered. Maybe she hadn't heard him, Weston thought. He returned to the table and left her an extra tip.

Once home, Weston decided he had better stay put until the sentencing. The river and Precious were a lot friendlier. Actually, he'd expected the worst from the townsfolk and was surprised when Sally had invited him to sit with her.

Precious hadn't eaten her morning food when Weston checked on her. He suspected she'd mated during her escape. He'd keep a close eye on her, maybe get the vet to come take a look. At some point, he'd have to find someone to look after her while he was in prison.

He probably should think about putting on the storm windows since he had free time, but the day was unseasonably warm, and the snow was melting. Maybe he could rent out his place during his prison term, and he began to think of what he should do to prepare the place for renters. People were always showing up at the Buckhorn asking for a place to rent in Northwood, rather than live in the city. They commuted back and forth to Superior or Duluth for work. He might even find someone who would care for Precious. Ole would have done it for nothing. He'd ask Sally to help with Evie—if she ever came back home.

He looked at the Eau Claire and longed for the thick haze of a hot summer evening where noodle nests of gnats pestered him before swarming off in another direction. Lured by the river, he hungered for more. During summer, the stream was riddled with rocks and boulders, but when fall produced rain, the Eau Claire swelled with the pride of a new power. That was when he loved it most. Seldom transparent, the river hid much, revealed less this time of year. With any luck, it offered a momentary glimpse below its surface by way of an overhead sun or a leaping trout now and then, but only if he were paying close attention.

He couldn't resist taking a few casts and grabbed his fly rod. Fall trout fishing wasn't the greatest, but it was a comfort just to wade the river again and feel its strength against his thighs. Since the storm, the river was high, and white spouts spurted skyward between two boulders like a faucet that had been left running. Water splashed and gurgled as though there had been no escape, no capture, no humiliation. The thought of prison disappeared from his mind as he tossed a fly to the opposite shore, downstream of the newly formed fountain. He didn't get a rise, so he cast upstream just beyond the boulders. No luck there either. It was the perfect time of day. The sun had set, and a glow in the sky over his shoulder highlighted the stream. He always figured when he couldn't see below the surface, fish couldn't see him either. A fly riding a ripple and then gently descending to the depths was all it took to center him. The perfect fly was irresistible to a trout waiting to feed, but he never knew what lurked below. High water and the storm had probably disturbed the fish patterns. About the time fishing got good, he'd be doing time. Then *he* would be the prey. Once word got out wherever he was incarcerated, convicts would devour him. He knew their tricks.

He missed Ole and knew he would be out here with him despite the mess Weston was in. On the other hand, he was glad Ole hadn't been around to witness his demise.

Weston felt the nudge. His adrenalin surged. He tightened the line and steered the fly ever so gently to one side. Then it struck. Weston lifted the pole and knew he had hooked a prize. The capture thrilled him. Excited as he was, he kept his composure and followed the rules. Not about to give into its predator, the fish leapt from its watery haven to a sunlit orbit. It arced for an eternity, transforming pain into ecstasy. He judged the trout to be about 24 inches. It was a sublime moment when a practiced performer was lured into a foreign atmosphere.

This pro wasn't about to give in. At the height of its summit, the fish flipped its head sending the bait into orbit. The fly's flight was equally impressive, circling more than once before landing. Weston held his breath and came back to earth only after the fish and the bait had completed their descent. He reeled in his line.

FORTY

JUDGE PEARSON ADJUSTS HIS horn-rimmed glasses, pushes a stray lock of grey hair from his forehead and repeats, "Is there anything you would like to say in your defense, Mr. Weston?"

"Yes, your Honor. I committed the crime of allowing a prisoner to escape, in fact, I forced it."

His eyes blur for the moment, and he's afraid he is going to faint. He's always taken responsibility for his actions, trusting his instincts. But how can he recognize truth when reality has failed him so miserably? He's been betrayed, tricked by the very words that spelled out the rules. His mental storeroom is overloaded, devouring him. He must be crazy. He sways. His lawyer grabs his arm. It takes all he can muster to stand erect.

"I lost control, your Honor."

Whispers gain momentum throughout the courtroom as the judge pounds his gavel.

"Silence in the courtroom." The judge pauses to clear his throat. He removes his glasses and rubs a hand over his bushy eyebrows before replacing his glasses and continuing. "Now then, Mr. Weston, I refuse to accept your guilty plea." Judge Pearson speaks in measured words. "As I see it," he says, "the rules let you down."

"But I'm guilty!" Weston explodes.

"Do not interrupt. In some ways the justice system is at fault," the judge continues. "You were expected to be invulnerable to do your job. Your need to control spilled into obsession, and you cracked under the pressure of seeing your daughter with the prisoner. Do you understand what I'm saying?"

"I think so, your Honor." The 'cracked under pressure' part hurts. For a moment he thinks he's back in church listening to the *Fish Catches Record Man* sermon, the one that was meant for everyone but him.

Weston looks down. A shaft of sunlight cuts across the floor blinding him. It never occurred to him that he could unknowingly head in a wrong direction. Had his life always been careening out of control? He deserves to go to prison.

Judge Pearson stares at him. "Mr. Weston?"

Weston cannot look him in the eye.

A commotion in the back of the courtroom causes everyone to turn. Evie bursts through the double doors, hair flying every which way as she shrugs off the police and races to her father.

Weston turns from her.

"Dad," she cries. "Dad, I gave myself up." Wrapping her arms about him, she presses her head against his chest.

Unable to resist, he clings to her.

Once again Judge Pearson sounds his gavel. "Order. Please be seated, young lady."

As Evie is peeled from him, Weston feels naked and weak, a stranger to his body. His legs buckle, and he drops to his knees. He is a clumsy absurdity.

"Don't judge yourself, Mr. Weston," the judge says, "I am here to do that."

Weston struggles to stand and lifts his head out of a long-term respect for the chain of command.

"You, Mr. Weston, are not being judged. You are many persons, depending upon who is seeing you—in addition to the one person you think you are. No, I am not judging you. My job is to judge your actions.

"Now," the judge's deep voice resounds, "on to the business at hand. Mr. Weston, I am convinced, based upon the testimony presented, that you acted out of frustration, caught between being a conscientious correctional official and a father.

"You have demonstrated trustworthiness during your impressive career as a correction officer and prison superintendent." He pauses. "You are innocent in the eyes of the law. Although it is out of my jurisdiction, I can, however, recommend to the State Correctional Authorities that your pension be honored in retirement. I absolve all guilt connected with the Court vs. Carl Weston. Court is dismissed." The judge raises his gavel.

"But your honor, I am guilty," Weston cries out. "You should throw the book at me!"

Holding the gavel aloft, Judge Pearson says, "Where's your compassion, Mr. Weston?"

"I don't understand."

"I mean compassion for yourself."

Weston is dumbfounded. He thought he got the pride thing. But compassion? It was bred out of him long ago.

The judge bangs his gavel twice.

"All please stand," the court clerk announces as the judge strides from the courtroom.

Weston slowly shakes his head as Evie jumps from the bench to Weston's side.

He wants to turn his back on her. Exhausted, he looks down at her and asks, "Where's Brand?"

"I don't know," she says. "He promised to turn himself in."

. Weston knows better than to swallow that line but decides not to say anything. He's suddenly tired of controlling the world. Maybe Brand had something in him that Evie saw, and he didn't.

Weston's lawyer pats him on the shoulder. "Nice job, Warden."

"Let's go, Dad," Evie whispers.

"Hang on," Weston says.

Weston lifts his head and stares out the rippled-glass windows in the old courtroom. He looks back on the treacherous landscape he's traveled for sixty years. His eye wanders downstream balancing on a smooth boulder then scans the snow-laden bank. Shoreline grasses part and darken, combed by a fierce wind. The river has marked his boundaries, pumping his blood through the forest floor.

He thought he would become wiser and braver as he aged. Now he feels soft and giddy as a child, sliding down an ancient river freezing and thawing between earth and air.

ACKNOWLEDGMENTS

The author wishes to thank the following people for facilitating the research for *Escape* which gives the book its authenticity: Len Fromholtz, Greg Polzin, Wes Carlson, Jerry Smith, Wendy Youngquist Katzmark, Joe Thayer, John Thayer, Loren Sloan, Mary Lou Bergman, Ron Kofal, and Barry Sigman.

In addition, thank you to the following loyal readers: Gloria Whelan, Beth and Ed Howard, Janet and Steve Moore, Peter Arcese, Kyrs Rollins, Barry Sigman, Sean McGillen, and Kelly Boll.